Hugh and Bess
A Love Story

Susan Higginbotham

Onslow Press

Hugh and Bess

A Love Story

Copyright © 2007 by Susan Higginbotham

ISBN: 978-0-6151-7187-6

Printed in the United States of America

To my readers

Acknowledgments

Writing a second novel, I have heard it said, is far harder than writing one's first. I wholeheartedly agree. My task here was made considerably easier by the people I encountered after I completed the predecessor to *Hugh and Bess*, *The Traitor's Wife*. To include everyone would be an impossible task, but I would particularly like to thank Alianore, who shares my fascination with the reign of Edward II and its aftermath and whose public blog and private e-mails have afforded me hours of stimulating conversation and encouragement. Author Brian Wainwright very kindly pointed out some blunders I as an American fell into with regard to forms of address. Martyn Lawrence generously sent me a copy of his dissertation on the Despenser family. Many others, on and offline, have touched my heart with their well wishes and their interest in the people of these novels.

As before, special thanks go to my husband, children, and parents.

Prologue

The Earl of Salisbury, William de Montacute, had been telling the same story since his eldest child was four years old. Over the years, it grew longer as the world acquired more Montacutes, and it might have assumed an embellishment or two or three, but it was told so often, and was so important in the Montacute annals, that it never needed a name. It was simply The Story.

Once, the story went, there had been a weak king, the second Edward. Not a bad man, not a cruel man, but one who would have been better off being almost anything than the king. (Yes, God made kings, but some might have been better off not being so. The Almighty's ways were inscrutable.) He had a knack for choosing friends whom everyone else in the kingdom hated, and none had hated his last friends, the elder Hugh le Despenser and his son the younger Hugh le Despenser, as much as did the king's own queen, the lovely Isabella. So much had she hated them that in 1326, having traveled from France, she had returned with an army, killed her husband's friends, forced the king from his throne in favor of his young son the third Edward, and shut the king away where he could never rule again.

Although the third Edward was still a mere boy, he might have ruled well with the help of his wiser elders until he grew to full manhood. But the beauteous Queen Isabella had not come to England alone. She had come with a cruel man, a greedy man, named Roger Mortimer, who would have liked to have been king himself if given half a chance. From the day he and the queen stepped ashore it was Roger Mortimer who had ruled England, taking as many lands and titles as he could grab, and treating the young king himself with no more respect than he might have shown one of his own pages. And less than a year after the second Edward had given up his crown, Roger Mortimer had had the old king killed. (William de Montacute would never tell the children how. The Montacute boys had found out, though, and chuckled about it nervously behind their hands. The Montacute girls were content to leave the matter be.)

And then Roger Mortimer—who had made himself the Earl of March—did another thing just about as wicked as that last. He led the king's kindly, naïve half-brother, the Earl of Kent, to believe that the second Edward was still alive. When the Earl of Kent fell into the trap, Mortimer had had his head cut off. (Here, all the Montacute children's eyes turned toward their companion, Joan of Kent, who had been little more than a baby when her father was killed and who found the story as interesting as did the Montacute children. If Joan of Kent was any indication, the unfortunate earl had been a very handsome man.)

But the demise of the Earl of Kent made all the children sit up straighter, for the best part of the story was to come—Papa's. Though Papa was a good decade older than the third Edward, who was only a lad of seventeen, he was fond of the young king and was distressed to see him being pushed aside by the wicked Mortimer and his poor, deluded mother. (William would never say anything bad about Queen Isabella; it would have hurt the king's feelings.)

"The king had a son the June after the poor Earl of Kent died," Papa would say, with another nod toward pretty Joan. "A sturdy, fine lad he was. It wouldn't have done for the king to be skulking around and having orders barked at him, not with his son looking toward him as an example. And Mortimer was growing worse every day. He'd walk side by side with the king, even. Let his servants eat with the king's. Remain seated when the king entered the room. And once he'd killed the Earl of Kent—the king's own uncle, you remember—no one knew who was going to be next. The king's other uncle? The Earl of Lancaster? The king himself? We knew we had to eat the dog, or the dog would eat us."

"And then you went to Nottingham Castle!" said Bess de Montacute.

"Then we all went to Nottingham Castle," agreed her father. He was taking his time now; his audience was sitting open-mouthed. "For a council meeting. I thought that was going to be my last day on earth. Mortimer had his spies, and I had a few of my spies, and the king had his spies, and all of us had been spying aplenty. First thing that morning, Mortimer summoned me and my mates in front of him. He knew we were getting tired of him. It was October of 1330, you see, and the king would be eighteen in a month. Mortimer asked us, one by one, what we were doing. All of us stayed silent—except for me. I told him that I would do nothing inconsistent with my duty to the king. Left him speechless for a moment or two, which was a feat where Roger Mortimer was concerned, I'll give myself that."

The children waited expectantly as their mama cast an admiring look at her husband.

"He wanted to have me arrested then and there, I knew, but couldn't think of a good reason to justify it, so he let me and the others go. And go I did, into the town; I thought it best to stay clear of the castle for a time. There I happened across a man named William Eland—or he happened across me. He knew what had gone on that morning, and he guessed what was in our minds. He told us about something only he knew about the castle."

"A secret passage," said young Will reverently.

"Right, a secret passage, all covered with bramble, but one that led straight into the castle. I knew then that a gift had been handed to me straight from God; it was now or never. So I got to the king through Eland; he stayed at the castle, you see, and had no difficulty finding an excuse to speak to his grace. And late that night, we climbed through the tunnel into the castle."

"It must have been damp," said Bess. "And full of spiders."

"Some as big as my hands put together, Bessie. Well. There they were in Mortimer's chamber: the queen and Mortimer and their cronies, meeting—deciding, we found out later, how to get rid of my friends and me. We came up the tunnel, made our way up a flight of stairs, and there we were by Mortimer's chamber. It would have pleased us to do without bloodshed, but Mortimer's man at the door attacked us with a sword, so we had to kill him. Shoved past him and ran into the room. Mortimer had an armed guard inside too; we had to kill him also. But we didn't have to kill Mortimer; him we arrested. When the sun rose that morning, the king announced he would rule on his own. And so he has, ever since. And though he and I were good friends before that, we're even better ones now. There's nothing I wouldn't do for the king, or him for me." William pointed to his belt proudly. "And that is why I am the Earl of Salisbury today, and your mama a countess."

"And why you children must marry suitably," their mother had started to add over the years, gently yet firmly. But none of the children paid much attention to this postscript, at first.

1

January 1341 to April 1341

Strictly speaking, Bess told herself, she was not eavesdropping on her parents, for she had been curled up in a window seat, half dozing, when they came in, and before she could say a single word, they had launched into a conversation that plainly was too important (and too interesting) to bear interruption. And she had been told many times not to interrupt; it was a bad habit of hers. So she would not do so now. Instead, she drew her feet up where they could not be seen and quietly rearranged the heavy drapes to screen herself more securely from view.

"The king himself proposed the marriage," her father had said when he first came into the room. "And there's nothing to be said against the man, Katharine. Everything for him, as a matter of fact. He's a good fighter. He's rich. He's the king's near kinsman and a great-grandson of the first Edward. So how could you possibly object? He'll make an excellent husband for her."

So it was true; her parents were at last arranging a marriage for Joan of Kent, who though her mother was still alive had been raised with the Montacute children and with the king's children after the wicked Mortimer had been hung at Tyburn. It was high time the girl got married, all of the Montacute household had been saying so. Joan was almost thirteen, less than a year younger than Bess, but unlike Bess, who at thirteen and a half still had simply a chest, Joan had breasts, unmistakable ones, even under the modest robes she and the Montacute girls wore. More than once Bess had heard her mother tell her brother Will that he should not stare at Joan's breasts. "I realize it is difficult not to, with them poking forward as they do," Katharine had said tartly. "But you must try. My, that girl needs to be married, and soon!"

Bess herself had been married several years ago to Giles de Badlesmere, soon after Papa became an earl and she had become a desirable match. Then after only a year of marriage—if one could count living with her parents while her grown husband lived on his estates as a marriage—Sir Giles had fallen ill, leaving Bess a widow at the age of eleven. Her husband had sent her gifts on occasion and had visited her several times, but she had known him little better than any of the other men who came to visit her parents, and though she dutifully prayed for his soul, his death had otherwise meant little to her. She was vaguely aware that she had been left quite prosperous by the brief union, and she had a sense that suitors had approached Papa about her now and then, but none had been quite right, it appeared. There seemed to be no great hurry, after all; she had just started her monthly courses a few months before, and her figure was still so far from womanly that had she put on her brother Will's clothes and hidden her waist-length, thick, dark hair, she could have taken service as a page.

But Joan was a different matter altogether, yet Mama did not appear happy. "Nothing wrong with him! His father executed as a traitor, his grandfather executed as a traitor, his great-grandfather killed fighting for Simon de Montfort against the king—"

"So, at least *he* wasn't executed as a traitor, Katharine. And the great-great-grandfather was quite respectable, I understand."

Bess's mother did not laugh. "I suppose one should feel pity for the man; he can't help his parentage, but what girl would want to call herself the wife of Hugh le Despenser?"

"Despenser wouldn't have suggested the match himself, I imagine. He knows full well of his family's disgrace and that some are loath to associate with him; it's probably what has kept him single all of these years."

"Indeed," said Katharine, finding a straw to grab upon. "He can't be young, is he, William?"

"He is two-and-thirty."

"Two-and-thirty! William, that's far too old for a girl of thirteen."

"Bess will mature soon. And Badlesmere was in his twenties himself, Katharine."

Behind the curtains, Bess gasped, covering her mouth just in time. *She* was to marry Hugh le Despenser?

SOON AFTERWARD, Bess's parents had left the room, and she had made her way back to the chamber she shared with Joan of Kent and her sisters just in time to be told that her father and mother wished to speak to her. She had been summoned to her mother's chamber, where Bess's parents had broken the news to her gradually, so much so that Bess, who had been worried lest she give away the fact she had been eavesdropping, had been almost lulled into believing she had misunderstood. So distressed had she been when she realized that she had heard them correctly that she had not had to feign shock. "I don't wish to marry him. I do not like him."

"Like him, Bess? You've never met him." Her father smiled tolerantly.

"I could not like a man from such a horrid family."

She had expected more help on this score from her mother, but Katharine, whatever her opinions might be in private, was a woman to stand publicly with her husband. "It is not for you to refuse this match, Elizabeth. You will marry him. You are a widow, after all; it is most suitable that you remarry."

"Why can't Joan marry him? Her father was beheaded too. They would have much more to talk about."

William's lip twitched upward, but he still managed to say testily, "Hugh asked for your hand, not Joan's. In any case, he would have asked in vain, because we have decided that Joan will marry your brother Will, quite soon as a matter of fact."

So now he can stare at her breasts all he likes, Bess thought, then remembered the matter at hand. "I don't *want* to marry him, Papa." She looked up into her father's face and gazed at him sadly with her large brown eyes, a trick that up to now had never missed with her father, though Bess to her credit had used it sparingly. "Please don't make me."

"I must, child. I cannot have you dictating to me whom you shall marry. I would not marry you to a man I did not esteem; you should know that. His father did disgrace his family's name, but Sir Hugh has done much to restore it. But I will allow you to sit with us when he comes to visit tomorrow or the next day. You will see for yourself that he will make a good husband for you, and you will get a chance to come to know him."

"And Hugh is a rich man," added Katharine. "You will be Lady of Glamorgan, and have many castles, you know. It won't be bad, I promise."

Nor, thought Bess, had she promised that it would be good.

BESS'S ONE CONSOLATION during the conversation with her parents had been that she would get to break the news to Joan of her own fate, but even here she was balked. "I have heard, Bess. My mother told me when she was visiting here the other day."

Queen Isabella and the wicked Mortimer had imprisoned the Earl of Kent's widow and children after the unfortunate earl was executed. After Mortimer was arrested, young Queen Philippa had taken an interest in the Earl of Kent's high-spirited little daughter, Joan, and she had spent most of her life with either the royal children or the Montacute children, or sometimes both, while still seeing her own mother and brother and sister often. She was lucky, Bess thought sourly, getting to marry her old friend and playmate Will instead of a stranger over twice her age and a traitor's son to boot. Yet Joan did not look any more happy over her marriage than Bess did over her own, Bess realized. "So why didn't you tell me? Don't you want to marry Will?"

"No."

"Why?"

"I've my reasons."

This had become Joan's favorite saying since she had started her monthly courses and developed those breasts of hers. "Well, they can't be very good ones. Will is your own age and pleasant and handsome, not some horrible old creature like I have to marry. And you will be Countess of Salisbury one day."

"Sir Hugh is my kinsman. My papa was his great-uncle. He's not old or horrible; I've met him." Joan fingered a russet curl. "And what if I don't want to be Countess of Salisbury, but plain Lady Joan?"

They sat side by side on the bed they shared in the girls' chamber, commiserating with each other. Then Joan said, "At least I won't have to bed with your brother just yet, as he's a mere boy. Will they make you bed with Sir Hugh, do you think? I daresay he's ready."

"They didn't say," said Bess.

"They probably won't just yet," said Joan. "Undress and I'll tell you what I think." Bess obeyed and Joan looked at her appraisingly. "You still don't have a bust, though I think you might have a little more than you did. No hips. Your hair's lovely but Sir Hugh won't care about hair. I wager they'll make you wait a year." She squinted at Bess as she hastened to dress again. "At least."

TWO DAYS LATER, a page arrived in Bess's chamber with the dreaded words, "My lady, the earl and the countess wish to see you in their chamber. Sir Hugh is with them."

Despite her best efforts, Bess could not find fault with her suitor's appearance. Hugh's face, though not strikingly handsome, was agreeable to the eye; his clothes were rich but not gaudily so; and his lean body, neither too short nor too tall, was that of a soldier, not that of a lingerer at dinner tables. His smile when Bess entered the room revealed good teeth and lit up his dark eyes. He bowed. "My lady."

"Sir."

"Your parents and I have been discussing the fact that we fear there may be a delay in us getting married. It seems that your first husband's mother was a Clare, and of course my mother was a Clare too, though I don't think the branches ever got on particularly well." He smiled at her again. "But nonetheless, for reasons I've never quite understood, that will require us to get a papal dispensation. You know what that is?"

"I am not a fool, Sir Hugh. Of course I know what one is."

"Yes, of course. I beg your pardon." Hugh had the look of a man getting up after a bad fall from a horse. "I don't think it will pose much of a difficulty, though, as the relationship is not a close one by any means, and for grounds I can tell the Pope that it is necessary to promote harmony between my family and yours. As my family was out of harmony with virtually everyone in England until recently, I'm probably not stretching the truth."

The Earl of Salisbury chuckled, and Hugh, back in the saddle, so to speak, continued, "Your parents have told me that you will be coming to live with me when we are married. I am very pleased to hear it. I must warn you that my furnishings are rather plain, as I have been single for so long, but I am sure that between you and your mother and my aunts and sisters we could get them looking nice very soon."

"I am entirely capable of choosing my own furnishings, Sir Hugh."

"Of course."

The earl shot his prospective son-in-law a look of commiseration.

"Must I share a bedchamber with you?"

"Elizabeth!" hissed her mother.

Hugh studied Bess, who for a horrid moment thought that he was going to ask her to strip, as had Joan. Then he said quietly, "I must leave that to your parents to decide for now, Lady Elizabeth, and I will abide by what they say. I know you are very

young still. I would not do anything to make you uneasy or en-
danger your health, for the world."

"Until she is a bit older I would ask that she have her own
chamber," said her father. "She has not really started to grow
yet, I think."

"Probably in a year or so," said her mother. Had she been
talking to Joan? Bess scowled at Hugh, though it was she who
had invited this embarrassing topic of her development, or lack
thereof. But he himself seemed glad to be off the subject and
was telling her parents that he would like to be married at
Tewkesbury Abbey, if it was agreeable to the Montacutes; it was
an abbey his late mother had taken a great deal of interest in before her death, and he was carrying out her plans to continue
renovating it. A horrid place full of dead Despensers, Bess supposed, but she put up no argument on the theory that one place
in which she married this man would be as bad as another. She
watched the fire moodily as the men segued into a talk about the
king's sudden return from Flanders the November before and his
difficulties with Parliament. Their talk was far less illuminating
than the fire, as Bess's father had been the prisoner of the King
of France until being released late in the previous year and therefore had missed quite a bit, and Hugh le Despenser preferred to
serve his king in war and to keep his mouth shut in peace, as he
put it.

At last the conversation ended, and then Hugh said the words
Bess had been dreading. "I was thinking that I might take Lady
Elizabeth riding for a bit, the weather being so fine at the moment?" He saw Bess's unenthusiastic face and added, "Perhaps
one of her sisters would like to join us."

Her parents agreed, and soon Hugh was helping her and her
ten-year-old sister, Sybil, onto their horses. He had evidently
prepared a great deal of horse talk for the occasion, for no sooner
than the girls were mounted than he began asking them how often they rode, where they liked to ride, what size horse each
preferred, what temperament of horse each favored, and so forth.
Bess answered him in as few words as possible, but Sybil, who

11

was evidently much taken with her prospective brother-in-law, was more forthcoming, so much so that Bess began to feel superfluous as the conversation began to turn away from her despite Hugh's obvious efforts to the contrary.

When Sybil and Hugh had at last exhausted the topic of horses, or ridden it to death as it were, Sybil asked, "Where shall you and Bess chiefly live, my lord?"

"Please feel free to call me Hugh, Lady Sybil. And you too, Lady Elizabeth. Hanley is probably the most comfortable of my castles for a lady, I think; it was the one my mother liked best. I spend a lot of time at Cardiff as well. I expect that Lady Elizabeth will find her favorites."

"Papa says you are rich, Hugh. How is that if your father died a traitor and lost his lands?"

"Sybil!" Bess hissed, concerned less with sparing Hugh's feelings than with the ill-breeding such a question surely showed. (Sometimes it was all too apparent that her father hadn't been an earl for all that long.) But she was curious enough to hope that Hugh answered.

Hugh said easily, "It's a fair enough question, I daresay. I was fortunate; my family's wealth came mainly from my mother's lands. She lost the best ones when Mortimer was in power, but when your father brought him down the king very kindly permitted her to have them back. She died several years ago, and I was her heir, of course. The king also was gracious enough to give me some of my father's and grandfather's lands too, but most of them are in the hands of the crown or in those of others, and always will be, I suppose. I've no cause for complaint. It could have been much different."

"It will be sad for you, getting married with no parents to see you," said Sybil earnestly. Bess could have swatted her.

"Yes, Lady Sybil, but there will be plenty of family to see me. I have eight living brothers and sisters, and several fine nephews, and my aunt Aline from my father's family. My aunt Elizabeth, my mother's sister, will come, I imagine. I don't know about my aunt Margaret; she never forgave my family for what happened in my father's day. Still, as her husband was made an earl along with your father, they may attend out of respect for him."

"I daresay many will attend out of respect for *my* father," Bess said loftily.

"No doubt," said Hugh a little stiffly.

They were saved from the necessity of further conversation by the rapidly graying sky, which made Hugh determine to turn back to Denbigh Castle, where the Montacutes had taken up residence for the time being. Their ride had been a meandering one, and Bess was surprised to see how easily Hugh retraced their path. "You must have been at Denbigh before, Sir Hugh," she surmised, remembering too late that she had exceeded the ration of words she had determined to speak to him.

"Plain Hugh, Lady Bess—Bess, if *I* may. You have your wits about you, I see. I do know it. It was my grandfather's for a while, and I came here a time or two while it was in his hands."

"He lost it when he was executed?" Bess felt a bad taste come into her mouth with the word "executed." What on earth would she tell their children about this man's relations?

"Precisely. But it hadn't been his for long. He gained it from Thomas, the late Earl of Lancaster, when he was executed; my grandfather lost it when *he* was executed; it went to Mortimer who lost it when *he* was executed; and then it went to your father. Good Lord, I've made it sound an ominous place, haven't I? I didn't mean to, sweetheart." He laughed. "It's a wonder the tenants can remember to whom to doff their caps, though."

They arrived at the stables. To avoid Hugh, Bess would have scrambled down from her horse unassisted, as she was perfectly capable of doing, but he was too quick for her and in a flash was off his own steed and standing next to hers. Bess stiffened as he helped her dismount; now that he had sneaked in this "sweetheart" of his, was a kiss next on his list? An embrace? But he handed her down as chastely as her own page might have done.

Sybil, however, had given her an idea, and as soon as Hugh left the next morning, she went to find her parents. "I thought

Sybil got on very well with Sir Hugh yesterday. Perhaps *she* could marry him?"

Katharine frowned at Bess, but her father laughed tolerantly. "Still trying to wiggle your way out of matrimony, Bess? It won't do, I tell you. I think Sir Hugh wants a lady who can be a proper wife to him sooner than Sybil could. And in any case, he likes you. He told me before he left how pretty and charming he had found you."

Bess found this to be deceit on Hugh's part, for she knew well she had not been charming, and she did not see how Hugh could have found her pretty. But it was clear that she had no more weapons at her disposal, so she resigned herself to her fate.

HUGH HAD BEEN RIGHT about a papal dispensation being necessary; the wedding would have to wait until after one was obtained, though with the king himself lending his support (Bess learned to her chagrin), its being granted was practically a foregone conclusion. No such obstacles barred Joan of Kent from marrying Will, however, and in early February, they became husband and wife.

Bess had been much dismayed to find that Hugh would be attending the wedding and would be seated beside her at the festivities, yet even her preoccupation with her own troubles could not prevent her from noticing the bride's odd behavior. Joan of Kent burst into tears twice in the time it took her ladies to dress her, a third time after she was all dressed, and a fourth time while she was riding in state to the ceremony. Standing at the church door with Will, she remained dry-eyed, but she looked like a deer surrounded by huntsmen. How could Will provoke such a reaction? Bess wondered. It was true that he was no great romantic figure for Joan—just plain old Will, whom she had known since she was a toddler—but what was wrong with marrying someone safe and familiar?

She was still puzzling over this at the wedding banquet when several courses into the feast, her father stood up and clapped for silence. After commenting gallantly on the beauty of his son's young bride (indeed, Bess noted enviously, there was not a male in the room who had not been gazing at Joan raptly at some time or the other), he lifted his cup and said, "And God willing, there will soon be another wedding in the Montacute family. Between my little Bess here and Sir Hugh le Despenser!"

There was an uneasy silence for a breath or two and Bess felt a twist of pity as she sensed Hugh tensing beside her. Then the king himself stood. "To Sir Hugh and Lady Elizabeth!" he said, smiling as suddenly the room resounded with cups clanking and hands clapping. "May they soon wed and prosper."

It was soon after this, when Will and Joan had gone off to live by themselves, albeit in separate chambers until they—or at least Will—matured a little, that the Countess of Salisbury called Bess to her. "Hugh has come up with an excellent idea. He would like you to spend some time with his aunt, Lady Elizabeth de Burgh, before you are married. She manages many estates, and there is much she can teach you."

"But you have taught me how to do that," protested Bess, noticing the unadorned "Hugh" with dissatisfaction. When had her mother melted so much toward Sir Hugh?

"To some degree, but our estates are small compared to hers, with her third of the Clare inheritance and her dower lands from her three husbands. And Hugh has his third of the Clare estates, plus what the king has allowed him of his own family's, plus yours. And it's only a matter of time before our men are off to war again, I imagine. You must be able to help manage all that land when your lord is away. Lady Elizabeth de Burgh will be able to teach you much that I cannot."

So in April, when all of the great lords of the land headed to Westminster to Parliament, Bess went to Usk in Wales, noting as she rode into the Burgh estates that not so much as a sheep appeared to be out of place. The handsome lady who greeted her in the great hall was no less tidy than her estates. After the usual exchange of civilities, she scrutinized Bess as closely as possible while staying within the bounds of politeness. "So you are to marry my nephew Hugh."

"Yes, my lady."

"Good. High time he got married, I'd say. You look as if you'll do well for him, too."

Bess tried to recall what Hugh had told her about his mother's younger sister. "She's been married three times, and has been a widow for nearly twenty years—her last husband was killed fighting against the second Edward and my father. Most men did fight against the king and my father at one time or another, I'm afraid; they weren't popular men. Well. In any case, she could have taken against us Despensers even after my father was dead, as did my aunt Margaret, but she didn't. She's been quite friendly to all of us, and I know she'll like you. You'll like her too. She's been running those endless estates of hers all by herself since she was only in her twenties, and if any man tried to propose marriage to her, she'd probably beat him senseless. She likes her independence, you'll find."

For the next few days Bess dutifully watched and listened as Elizabeth de Burgh met with her councilors, sat in on her manor court proceedings, received visits from her tenants, reviewed her account books, chose her household's midsummer livery, entertained her daily stream of visitors, and even managed to spend some time falconing. Just observing her exhausted Bess. "Of course, Hugh will be doing many of these things when he is on his estates, Bess, but mark my words, he won't be on them long. The king is itching to get back at the head of an army, and your Hugh's not one to oppose his wishes, I've noticed. If the king wants him to fight somewhere, he'll be there."

"You think him servile?" Bess said, a little miffed.

"No, I think him a man of sense, given his background. How much do you know about Hugh?"

"Not much. His father and grandfather were dreadful men, I've heard, and were hung."

"That's putting it mildly in both respects. The father was the worse by far. He extorted land from me and from dozens of others; he took to piracy at one point; and he was a sodomite—with the king no less. Don't blush; you're better off hearing this from me than from one of your tenants someday. He had the second Edward—my uncle—under his thumb, not that the king didn't want to be there. Queen Isabella stood this for as long as she could until the king like a fool sent her to France to negotiate with the French king. After she'd been there a while she told him she would never come back while the Despensers were in power. But come back she did, with an army, and both Despensers were executed. I'd not speak to your husband on the subject if I were you. The grandfather was hung, beheaded, and cut in bits and fed to the dogs. His father was stripped naked, hung on a fifty-foot gallows, drawn, beheaded, and quartered. And emasculated as well. Most thought it his just deserts, given his doings with the king."

"Good Lord," breathed Bess. "Where was Hugh?"

"Caerphilly Castle, where he and the late king and his father had gone to stay a while, trying to raise troops against the queen. That's where he saw his father for the last time—he and the king left there like the blockheads they were to wander around Wales and were captured—and that's where Hugh remained long afterward. You've not got a coward for a husband, that's for certain. Hugh was just eighteen at the time. He and its constable held the castle for months, long after his father and grandfather had been executed, long after everyone else in the country had gone to the queen's side, long after the second Edward had agreed to give up the crown to his son. They finally surrendered it on the condition that Hugh's life be spared, and it was, of course, or we would not be talking as we are now, but Mortimer made sure that he was kept the crown's prisoner for over four years. Even after your father toppled Mortimer, Hugh stayed in prison for months afterward. I think the king was a bit nervous that he might be out for vengeance. But he's been nothing but loyal to the king, and he's served him well in his wars."

"Everyone admires him as a solider, I know. What is he like as a man?"

17

Elizabeth shrugged. "He was a good son to my sister, and he looks after his brood of brothers and sisters—there's eight living besides him—as he should. He seems to get on well with everyone, and I'm fond of him. He's even apologized to me and others for what his father did, although I never held what his father did against him, or at least I hope I did not do so. But I confess I don't know much of what goes on in his mind. That is for you to find out, my child."

2

October 1326 to June 1341

His father's confessor had been praying to St. Anne mightily for a favorable wind to push them to Lundy Island and from thence to Ireland, but for reasons known only to St. Anne herself, she was unwilling to oblige. Instead, the ship on which the second Edward and his entourage were traveling drifted even farther in the direction of Cardiff. Hugh turned to his father. "Maybe we should put in at Cardiff. Or try another saint?"

His father put out a hand; for a moment Hugh thought he was going to strike him. "Keep your mouth closed, boy, if you've nothing intelligent to say. It's not the time for making one of your fool jests."

Hugh recoiled as if he actually had been hit. He had always thought that his father liked his humor. But his father had a price of two thousand pounds on his head, which Hugh supposed might be affecting his temper. Not to mention having been at sea for five days since they had taken ship at Chepstow. He muttered, "I beg your pardon, my lord."

To his surprise, his father's face softened. He put a hand on Hugh's shoulder. "But you may be right." Letting his hand linger where he had placed it, he stared out toward the water. "Christ, I wish we hadn't left your grandfather in Bristol. It's full of our enemies."

"Grandfather will hold Bristol Castle fast," said Hugh confidently. His remark earned him a smile from the king, coming back from an exchange with the captain. Hugh dropped his eyes, taken aback. He had been in the king's household since he was a young boy, but recently he had heard odd rumors here and there about what the king and his father were to each other, and since then he had not felt entirely at ease with Edward, as he once had. Not that there could be any truth in the rumors, Hugh hastened to reassure himself, but just the fact that they were there . . .

"My son does have a point," Hugh's father said. Hugh raised his head again. He had made a point? "We're of no use where we are, hoping for a favorable wind. We're headed toward Cardiff. Let's disembark there. At least we can do something for ourselves once we land, better than we are now. You've friends in Wales still. We'll work from there."

Edward nodded, then smiled at Hugh again. "Clever lad."

Clever? It was not as if they had a great deal of choice in the matter, thanks to the contrary wind. But anything, Hugh thought, would be better than staying on this boat.

The decision having been made to put in at Cardiff, the wind shifted and for a time seemed determined to start blowing them in the opposite direction, but at last it turned again and they arrived at Cardiff Castle. It was the Despensers' own castle thanks to the lands that had come to Hugh's mother, but Hugh soon realized that the family was clearly not welcome. The staff went about their duties with a silence that was not respectful but sullen, and the summonses the king and Hugh's father sent out for men to join them against the queen went unanswered. Even the seagulls flapping around off Bristol Channel appeared reluctant to commit themselves, alighting on one of the castle's turrets for only a second or two before taking wing again.

Hugh, trying to help his father and the king in sundry ways and wondering if his presence was of much use at all, had some time to consider the matter and to talk to some of the garrison about it. After a few ales late one night had loosened some of the men's tongues, the name Hugh kept hearing was Llywelyn Bren, who'd led an uprising in the area some years ago, when Hugh had been a mere lad. Llywelyn had been taken to the Tower—indeed, his wife and children were still there, now under the care of Hugh's mother—and then removed by his father, who'd had him hung, drawn, and quartered at this very castle. It never should have happened, the garrison told Hugh, as the man had been promised his life in exchange for his surrender; Hugh's father had taken it upon himself to execute the man anyway. The locals hated his father for this act and had not forgotten it. Hugh le Despenser the younger was living in a world of dreams, the men of the garrison said, if he thought the men of Cardiff would come to his aid.

Hugh kept this information to himself, doubting that it would be a topic his father would relish discussing. Instead, he went on helping as he had been helping, keeping up the pretense that their efforts would be repaid. But his father must have been thinking along the same lines, for in late October, he and the king decided to move to Caerphilly Castle. The populace there might not be any less hostile, he heard his father telling the king, but at least the castle itself was better fortified than Cardiff. If, his father hastened to add, things came to that.

So the tiny court moved itself to Caerphilly. Built by Hugh's maternal grandfather, the red-haired Gilbert de Clare, it was Hugh's boyhood favorite of all his family's castles. It was huge and sprawling, full of hiding places for a lad, and Hugh felt a return of his old affection for it when they passed within its gates. His father's spirits had risen too, for he had spent a great deal of money some months ago in renovating Caerphilly's great hall, even hiring the king's own carpenter, and was glad of the chance to show off the result to Edward. "Hurley did himself proud, don't you think?"

"It's magnificent," said the king. "If only Gilbert the Red could see it now."

"Judging from the ones I have, the man wasn't much on beautifying his castles, just fortifying them. I doubt he'd approve." Hugh le Despenser the younger grinned at his son.

"Your mother will, though. She was born here, you know. Well, not smack in the middle of this hall, of course. In one of the chambers over there." He pointed toward a wing abutting the great hall. "I've had work done there too. Next time your mother comes to stay, she'll have a chamber fit for a queen."

There was a rather awkward silence, which Hugh inadvertently made worse by glancing up at one of the corbels below the great hall's roof rafters. It was a figure of Queen Isabella, wearing a magnificent stone crown. His father's eyes followed his. "It seemed like a good idea at the time," he said ruefully. "Anyway, the king's over here."

Edward chuckled. "Don't look so distressed, Hugh. We'll say the queen is a representation of my mother. Why, I think I even see the resemblance now that I think of it."

His father grinned. "And here's me, and there's my sweet wife. The heads were all Hurley's idea, in any case. I shall find it strange to have a meal with oneself gazing down upon oneself."

They had finished admiring his father's improvements and were sitting down to eat when a man entered the great hall. Though the man was not in livery, Hugh, his eighteen-year-old eyes sharper than his father's or the king's, recognized him from a distance. "Father? Isn't he one of Grandfather's men?"

"Yes." His father rose and met the man as he crossed toward the high table where they had been sitting. "Man, have you news from Bristol?"

"Yes, my lord. My lord—"

"Yes? Speak out."

"It is bad news, the worst. The Earl of Winchester surrendered Bristol Castle to the queen's forces. He had no choice; the garrison would no longer fight for him. He held out for six days nonetheless, but—"

"Where is he? Is that whore holding him prisoner? Edward! We must save him."

"My lord, it is too late. The earl was tried as a traitor the very afternoon of his surrender. He was condemned to death by a council convened by the queen and her paramour. The sentence was carried out the next morning." The man crossed himself. "The earl died two days ago, my lord."

Hugh, along with the king, had joined his father in the middle of the hall. He saw his father lurch to the side and into the king, who kept him from collapsing. It was Hugh himself who asked, "How?"

"Beheaded, Master Hugh." He hesitated. "They dragged him through the streets and hung him first. The whoresons who had the arranging of it made him wear his surcoat with his arms reversed. His head was sent to Winchester. His body was put back on the gallows. It was still hanging there when I left Bristol."

Hugh's father, still propped up by the king, was breathing harshly. It was the only sound in the great hall. Hugh, standing on his other side, took his hand. "Come, Father. Let me take you to your chamber."

"No." His father managed to stand upright. "No. I need— I must—"

He staggered out of the hall. Hugh would have followed his father, but the king, a powerfully built man, stopped him merely with a touch of his arm. "Best leave him alone for a time, Hugh."

"But he's distracted, your grace."

The king shook his head. "I know your father well. He needs time alone. When the time is right, I will come to him."

"When? Tonight when he lies in bed?"

Hugh could not believe what had come out of his own mouth, and he had said it loudly enough that the words echoed through Caerphilly's great hall. He waited for the king to knock him to the floor. Instead, Edward said, "I am forgetting that the Earl of Winchester was your grandfather. I grieve for him too. He was my friend in my father's court when I had almost no others, one of the most faithful men I ever knew. Something in you has always reminded me of him." He turned to the earl's man. "Tell me of my daughters and Lady Hastings."

Lady Hastings was his aunt Bella, one of his father's sisters. The king's daughters had been in her care at Bristol. Hugh waited long enough to hear the man inform the king that his daughters were safely in the queen's household and that Lady Hastings had been escorted to her dower lands on the day after her father's execution. Then, unable to hold back his sickness any longer, he ran from the great hall and vomited in the nearest bush. Finding himself alone, he heaved himself to his feet. He made his shaky way to his own chamber and huddled in the window seat.

Up until now, he'd dismissed the queen's invasion as an annoyance that could be got over, much like the time a few years back when his grandfather and his father had each been sent into exile by their enemies. His father had taken to piracy, his grandfather had gone to Bordeaux. Each had come back safe and well, and their enemies had been vanquished. So Hugh had thought would happen this time.

But all of their enemies had not been vanquished. Roger Mortimer had been left alive. And he and the queen together had killed Hugh's sixty-four-year-old grandfather—who had never been their chief foe. It was Hugh's father who was the queen's quarry, and there were fewer than a hundred people and Caerphilly Castle standing between him and the queen. Probably there would soon be fewer. Men had left the king's household at Cardiff, and now that Hugh's grandfather was dead, more might find it prudent to desert.

How could he have been so foolishly optimistic?

It was best, perhaps, not to think just now about how much he had loved his grandfather and would miss him. Instead, he knelt and prayed for the Earl of Winchester's soul. Then he prayed for their own skins.

His father did not reappear until the next morning. He had obviously not slept the night before, for there were dark circles under his eyes and he was wearing exactly what he had worn the previous day. The king, who a servant later told Hugh had spent the entire night sitting up with him, looked scarcely better. Yet the two of them made some pretense of normality, sending out yet more summonses that went unanswered. Overnight the household had shrunk even more. Hugh, waiting the next morning for shaving water that never came, discovered that his own page was one of the deserters. He'd taken off with his father, one of the king's household knights.

On All Hallows' Eve, the last of the royal clerks disappeared. With the exception of the garrison at Caerphilly and a few stray servants, the second Edward's court was down to a dozen men.

Several nights later, Hugh was shaken awake. "Father?" he muttered.

His father sat on the bed beside him. Coming to full consciousness, Hugh was not all that surprised to see him there. Since the Earl of Winchester's death, Hugh the younger could be seen wandering around Caerphilly at all hours. He had also virtually stopped eating, usually doing no more than rearranging the meat on his plate. "I came to tell you that we are leaving Caerphilly tomorrow morning. The king and I and a few others."

"Why?"

"The king thinks we can raise some support if men see him in person, rather than staying behind these castle walls. He may be right. And there's always the possibility that we might make it yet to Ireland." He fiddled with a ring on his finger. "Anyway, it's worth a try, I suppose."

"So where will we go next?"

"Not you. You're staying here."

"Father?"

"The king's leaving a great deal of money here. We need someone to guard it." His father's shoulders slumped. "Do you know what that whoreson the Earl of Leicester did? He and his men were supposed to be joining your grandfather to help guard against the queen's invasion. Instead they seized the money he'd brought to Leicester Abbey for safekeeping. If he'd only kept faith—" He shook his head. "Anyway, that's our plan. Between you and John de Felton, Caerphilly will be in good hands. I know you're capable of defending it."

"Thank you, Father."

His father shrugged. "Who knows, perhaps the king is right and we'll soon defeat the queen. In which case it'll be high time to find you a pretty, rich bride. All else being equal, who would you like? A blonde or a brunette? Not all that many redheads like your mother."

"A dark brunette," Hugh said, thinking of the silver-blond queen.

So was his father. "Aye, we've had enough of the fair Isabella, haven't we? Very well, a brunette she shall be. With a magnificent bosom."

Hugh blushed, remembering a particularly buxom fishmonger he'd admired at the Tower just a few weeks before. "I didn't realize I was so unsubtle."

"You are, but I'd have you no other way." Hugh's father managed a half smile, then stood. Hugh, following suit, realized with a start that he was a couple of inches taller than his father. Long accustomed to having to look down to speak to his petite mother, he must have only recently gained this height over his father. "Hugh . . ."

"Father?"

"If—if anything goes awry, look after your mother and the children."

"Of course, Father."

"And look after yourself. Don't do some of the fool things that I did." His father sighed and headed toward the door. "We'll be ready to leave at first light tomorrow."

And so they were, accompanied by an entourage far smaller than most royal hunting parties Hugh had seen. The king smiled at him as they mounted their horses. "High time you were knighted, Hugh. When I come back I'll do it. I'd do it now but you deserve more ceremony."

In spite of Hugh's misgivings, his spirits lifted. Sir Hugh! "Thank you, your grace."

"My pleasure."

Astride his own chestnut horse, his father reached over and ruffled Hugh's hair, a gesture he had not used since Hugh was a small boy. "God keep you, son."

"God keep you," Hugh echoed. From a guard tower a few minutes later, he stared at the king's party as they rode away from Caerphilly Castle, until at last he could see them no longer.

Weeks passed, during which Hugh and his companions at Caerphilly heard only rumors, most of them contradictory and none of them readily verifiable, about the whereabouts of his father and the king. Then toward the end of November, Hugh, preparing for bed, responded to a knock on his door and found John de Felton, the castle constable. "There is news at last of your father and of the king. News from one whose information can be relied upon."

"Yes?"

"The last rumor we heard was true; the king and Sir Hugh were captured not far from Llantrisant. The king has been taken to Kenilworth, where he will be kept in honorable captivity. Master Hugh, it grieves me beyond measure to tell the rest. Your father was taken to Hereford. On the day before the feast of St. Catherine, he was executed."

November 24, less than a month after his grandfather had been killed on October 27. Hugh felt himself begin to shake. Trying to regain some mastery over himself, he said, "He was used as they did my grandfather?" He saw Felton hesitate. "Tell me!"

"They used him—as he did Llywelyn Bren." *Drawing, hanging, disemboweling, beheading, and quartering.* Felton put his hand on Hugh's shoulder, but nothing he could do stopped the world from whirling around, and something in Felton's face made Hugh realize that he was still holding something back. After a while he said, "I hesitate to tell you the full story, but it would be an ill thing if you were to hear it from a foe instead of a friend."

"Yes. Let me hear it."

He listened as Felton, speaking as gently as he could, told him a tale of horror upon horror. His father, hoping to cheat the queen of his execution, starving himself from the time he was taken to the time he was executed at Hereford. His father, crowned with nettles, made to ride in chains from Llantrisant to Hereford on the meanest mount that could be found, hooted by the crowd and pelted with dung and garbage in each town through which the procession passed. His father, finally reaching Hereford, being stripped naked for the amusement of the by-standers and having admonitory scripture verses etched onto his skin. His father being dragged by four horses to a fifty-foot gallows, his man-at-arms Simon de Reading being hung below him. His father not only being disemboweled while he was conscious, but emasculated as well.

A silence fell. When Hugh next heard Felton's voice next to his ear, it was strangely far off. "Shall I send the chaplain to you, Master Hugh?"

"No. Leave me."

"Sir, I don't think—"

"I said leave me!"

"Sir—"

"Leave me, damn you!" He added, "Have someone bring me some wine. Plenty of it."

Felton slowly left the room. Some minutes later, a man arrived with the wine. Hugh shooed him out, seated himself on the window seat, and drank two large cupfuls rapidly. Two more cups followed in quick succession, yet poor as his head for wine had always been, the picture in his mind of his father being hacked to pieces was as vivid as before.

Someone knocked on his door, then called his name. Hugh paid the caller no mind, and soon he heard the sound of retreating footsteps. Two more cups, and the knock sounded again. "Get the hell away," he called. He knocked the cup over and stared at it stupidly.

"Master Hugh?"

The voice was a female one. After a moment, Hugh stumbled to the door and lifted the bolt. When the door swung open, he found himself staring at the castle laundress, Alice. She was in her forties, but when they had first arrived at Caerphilly, Hugh, missing the wenches he had enjoyed visiting in London, had wondered if she would do as a bedmate in their absence; she looked as if she might still have considerable lust in her. Then the world had turned upside down with the death of his grandfather, and he'd not thought of Alice again except as a source of clean shirts. "Ah, I was right. You were brought up too well for you to refuse a woman."

"They tormented him. They cut his—"

"I know, lamb. Come."

She held out her arms and he stepped into them, then sank to his knees and began sobbing into her skirts, at first quietly, then harshly. Alice eased herself down to his level and patted him on the back as he huddled against her weeping.

His stomach sent a warning in just enough time for him to turn and heave onto the rushes the wine he had gulped. Again and again he retched while Alice supported him. "Please don't tell the garrison," he muttered when he could finally speak again.

"I won't. Come, let's put you to bed."

Despite her gender, Alice through years of dragging washing around was easily as strong as Hugh. She hauled him to his feet as summarily as if he were a recalcitrant sack of laundry, mopped his face with a towel, stripped him to his drawers, and assisted him into his bed. Too weak and exhausted to protest at the intrusion, Hugh heard her open the door and murmur to someone outside, then heard the sound of someone sweeping up the soiled rushes and scattering fresh ones in their place. The sound had ceased, and Hugh had almost gone to sleep when he felt someone climb into bed next to him and touch his shoulder. Hugh blinked. "*Alice?*"

"Don't be daft, lamb, my days for *that* are long gone. I'm here to keep you company. With all the grief you're carrying, you shouldn't be alone tonight. Just lie here and sleep."

She gathered him closer to her. Alice's ample bosom was as sweet and as comforting as his childhood nurse's had been, and soon Hugh had fallen asleep upon it just as he had on his nurse's when something had gone wrong in his small world so many years ago.

When he awoke at last, the sun was high in the sky and Alice had left the bed. Rolling over and parting the bed curtains, he saw her sitting on a stool and glaring at his cloak, which she was brushing. "Alice?"

"Ah, there you are. That fool page of yours had no idea of how to treat your clothes, Master Hugh. This hasn't been properly brushed for months, I'll wager. You're well rid of him, I say."

"That's good." He hesitated. "Thank you, Alice. For last night."

She smiled at him. "Sometimes only a woman will do for a man, and not in the usual way."

He slowly sat up and ran a hand over his throbbing head. "Once I'd heard that rumor, I suppose I knew in my heart that it was true. And I knew that if they did catch him, there'd be no hope, not after they executed my grandfather. But to die like that—" He shuddered.

"Best not think of it, or you'll be getting yourself in the same shape you were last night. And you've other things to think of now. Your own head, mainly."

Hugh unconsciously ran his hand along his neck. "I wonder if they'd kill me," he said almost detachedly.

"Why not? They killed Simon de Reading, what for no one knows except that he was loyal to your father to the end. I suppose you've not heard about the Earl of Arundel?" Hugh shook his head. "They beheaded him the day after your father was captured. Him and two of his followers. All he did that anyone can think of was to marry his son to your sister and get some of Mortimer's lands."

"Christ." Hugh crossed himself. He slid out of bed and looked about for his clothes.

"Shall I call a man for you? I can undress a man a lot better than I can dress him."

"I've been managing on my own." He took the newly brushed clothes that Alice handed to him and began pulling them on. From behind his shirt he asked, "I don't know what to do. Stay here? Flee abroad?"

"The garrison was talking over your situation last night before I came to you. Most seemed to think that you should stay right here. Even if you were to dress in borrowed clothes and hide your face, the queen's men were bribing the people around here very generously when your father and the king were hereabouts. They'd have an eye out for you, and you favor your father a great deal. You could travel by night and hide by day, I suppose, but every man around would be combing his stables for you once word got out that you were at large. Here at least you can hold them off for a time."

Hugh winced. "My head aches too much to follow that, but I think I agree." He bent to retrieve the wine cup from where it had fallen the night before. Turning it in his hands as if he were reading his fortune in it, he said, "I know John de Felton will be loyal, but what will that count if the garrison deserts like my grandfather's did? Do you think they'll stay?"

"Only one way to find out."

"Even if they desert me, I'll stay as long as I can." Hugh looked at the doorway where his father had stood just a few weeks before, a lifetime ago. "I'll be damned if I let the queen complete her collection of Hugh le Despensers." He winced again as a jab of pain shot through his head. "Though I'm not sure I'd mind at the moment."

The garrison did not desert him. When the queen's forces arrived just hours later to seize the castle and Hugh, they found the gates shut up against them. Several times over the next few months the queen and Mortimer tried to entice the garrison with a pardon, expressly excepting Hugh's life, but they continued to resist the royal forces, even when the second Edward resigned his throne to his young son and all hope of resistance seemed futile. Hugh often wondered what had kept the garrison so loyal. Had it been regard for Felton or merely an abhorrence of seeing a man as young as he die on the scaffold? Or had it been respect for Hugh himself? Whatever their reasons, it was the men of the garrison who allowed him to hold out until mid-March, when the nominal king offered yet another pardon. This time, Hugh was promised that his own life would be spared. Knowing that no better offer would be forthcoming and that even these men's loyalty had its limits, he surrendered Caerphilly Castle and watched in its great hall, under guard, as Felton and the rest of those who had stayed true to him filed outside to freedom. Even a tearful Alice was with them, having left Hugh a pile of clean, crisp linen shirts to remember her by.

Then they were all gone, and it was just him and his captors. The commander of the besieging forces, William la Zouche, had treated Hugh kindly and considerately when taking him into custody, but not all of his men were so well disposed toward him, Hugh found when Zouche left the room. "Take a look around you, Despenser," said one of the guards as they prepared to lead Hugh to the far-off chamber in which he would be kept as the crown's prisoner. He was a young man, not much older than Hugh, and he had the look that Hugh would come to know well over the next few years: the look of someone who had realized that he was free to treat Hugh just as he pleased. The guard waved to encompass the splendor of the great hall. "You might never see this again, you know."

Hugh looked up at the corbel of his father and felt the ache in his chest that had never quite left it since the news had come. "If only he'd known," he said. "He could have spared himself the investment."

The guard glared. "Think you're amusing, Despenser? Shut your trap."

So began the next four years of his life.

HUGH SAT UP IN BED and, as usual, looked around him before arising. Though it had been nearly ten years since he had been the crown's prisoner, he still felt the need every morning to check his surroundings to assure himself that he was a free man. The need was even more compelling on occasions like this one, when he'd awakened from one of his bad dreams. They all ended the same way, with the sight of what he'd been spared in life: his father hanging naked in the air before being cut down, castrated, disemboweled, beheaded, and quartered. Then the queen's men came for Hugh himself with their noose.

He took a couple of deep breaths, reminding himself that all this was in the past and that he had nothing to fear. His own life was a good one. He was healthy, rich, and still relatively young, with no great sins on his head. He had led men in battle with success and was on reasonably good terms with the king, though they would never be intimates; in any case, his father had been so close to *his* king that this would probably have to suffice for whole generations of Despensers. He had no enemies, personal ones at least; if—or, to be more accurate, when—he died, it might be violently at the thrust of a French or a Scottish sword, but it would be a honorable death in battle, the death of a knight.

And what was he doing thinking of death anyway, when he was quite content, except for one thing?

He lay back again, taking more comfort in his surroundings. There was his familiar carved bed with the coverlet of material his mother had chosen for him. There was the pleasant feel of fine linen sheets against his bare skin; in prison, he'd always slept fully clothed, feeling too vulnerable and often too cold to do without his garments. If he parted the heavy bed curtains that matched the coverlet, he would see he was in his familiar chamber at Hanley Castle, overlooking the River Severn. Stretched out by the fireplace would be his favorite dog; Hugh could hear him having his nightly scratch. Although the dog's presence in his chamber at night violated every principle of civilized living his chamberlain held dear, Hugh let the animal stay; the four years he'd spent as a captive without friends had made him appreciate the ones he had now, human or canine.

The most reassuring sight, however, was that immediately to his right: Emma, sleeping beside him. No; not sleeping now. She was awake and put her arms protectively around him. He was still shaking, he realized; he must have screamed himself awake as he did on occasion.

"It's early, Hugh," she said gently. "Go back to sleep now. All is well."

But it wasn't, of course. That very day, Emma was going to leave him.

HE'D FIRST MET EMMA when they were each ten or so, not long after his mother had come into her third of the Clare inheritance, a third, he had become acutely conscious, that would someday be his own. His father was full of schemes to make his share an even larger one, but Hugh as he rode his horse through the family's new lands, exploring his surroundings, was cheerfully unaware of these ambitions, much less worried about to what they would lead.

On a fine day in early spring, he'd been riding off a heavy dinner when he came to a rutty area, too treacherous to go through at a fast pace. As he reined in his horse, he saw a flash of blue at a distance. Drawing closer, he saw that it was the cloak of a girl of his own age. Walking on a tree that had fallen across a stream, she was balanced as precariously as the acrobats he'd seen at court. Unlike the acrobats, she was encumbered by her gown and cloak, the skirts of which she had to hold with both hands to keep from tripping her up. Still, she was making it across the stream, though so slowly that Hugh, realizing that he had been holding his breath, had to let it out. As he did, his horse took a step forward and snapped a twig underneath its feet. With a yelp, the girl swung sideways, made a vain attempt to right herself, and fell into the stream with a prodigious splash.

Hugh scrambled down from his horse and reached the bank as the girl rose from the shallow water, dripping from her head to her toes. Somewhat disappointed that he would not have the chance to heroically save her life, he gave her his hand, but she ignored it and stepped onto the bank with as much dignity as she could muster under the circumstances. Her eyes, Hugh saw, were blazing, and they were also mismatched, one blue and one brown. "Did you make that noise?" He could only nod. "Oaf!"

"You were a fool to try to walk across it."

"I do it all of the time! How was I to know some idiot boy would make a racket?"

"If a little noise like that scares you so easily, you should have stayed on the bank where a girl belongs."

Having reached a verbal impasse for the time being, they glared at each other until Hugh remembered the chivalrous training he was receiving: a knight did not let a lady, even a peculiar-looking one who looked as if she might claw him with her nails, shiver in the cold while he enjoyed a warm cloak. Hugh took his off and handed it to her. "Here. It'll warm you a little."

"That's useless. My wet clothes will only get it wet too." She put it on, however, and Hugh saw her expression change when she realized from the fur inside how costly it was. Her face turned scarlet. "You—You must be—"

"Your new lord's son," said Hugh, thoroughly enjoying her discomfiture. "His *eldest* son," he added, doubling his pleasure as he saw her turn even redder. "There's Hugh le Despenser the elder, my grandfather; Hugh le Despenser the younger, my father; and me, Hugh le Despenser the Oaf." He considered adding that she was in his family's deer park, where she had no business, but decided to reserve this point for later.

"I—" She curtseyed. "I beg your pardon. I am shortsighted." She began to slide the cloak off. "I must go. Thank you for the cloak."

She was openly shivering, and wherever she lived, it would take her a while to get there. Probably letting the smart-mouthed wench catch her death of cold would be unchivalrous too; a

35

knight's life was not always an easy one. "That's silly; you'll freeze. Keep it on. Get on my horse and let me take you to the castle. Someone can find some dry clothes for you to borrow and bring you home." Whose clothes he could not imagine; though the girl was tall for her age, she was so skinny that his mother's robes would hang on her, and his oldest sister's robes would barely reach past her knees. He decided to leave that dilemma up to the womenfolk.

The girl was too cold to argue, it seemed. By the time Hugh got her on his horse, she was shivering so hard that she could hardly stay on without his assistance. Hugh pulled her closer to him on the saddle and gathered the cloak more tightly around her, nobly conquering his distaste for the females of the human species and their surefire way of spoiling perfectly good rides with their falling-into-water antics. A boy, he knew, would have stayed on the stupid tree. He heaved a martyred sigh and clucked at his horse.

At Hanley Castle, the servants took one look at the girl, now almost blue with cold, and hustled her upstairs to his mother's chamber, where she was wrapped in blankets and put in front of a fire. (Someone also took the trouble to ask her name, which Hugh certainly hadn't.) Though Emma, as she turned out to be, soon looked warm and comfortable, the occasional minatory sneezes she let out alarmed Hugh's mother, who to Hugh's utter disgust ordered that instead of being sent home straightaway, she be put to bed in his sisters' chamber and kept at the castle overnight, a message having been sent to her parents accordingly. Hugh comforted himself with the notion that Emma's sharp tongue would irk her companions and that she would be in high disgrace when morning came.

Instead, when the children broke their fast the next morning with watered-down ale and bread, Hugh discovered that overnight, his sisters had become devoted to Emma, who was several years older than Isabel, the oldest of the Despenser girls. Joan was too young to do much more than gaze worshipfully at Emma, but Isabel was a different matter. Already she and Emma had entered into a few of the private jokes that girls were so fond of, for they said things that were absolutely not humorous at all and laughed at them as heartily as if the king's jester had been putting on a command performance. Isabel had contrived to give Emma one of her girdles and would have given her one of her best jewels if Emma had not had the wisdom to suggest that Isabel's mother should be consulted. Worse, though Isabel and Emma whispered when they said it, Hugh distinctly heard the word "oaf" when they looked in his direction. Both of his sisters were in tears when Emma, resplendent in her dried and brushed clothes and her new girdle, left (not on a dung-wagon as Hugh had hoped, but on Isabel's own palfrey and escorted by a page). Only through promising to return in a few days to visit did Emma stem the flood of emotion.

Eleanor, Hugh's mother, was no better than her daughters. Several times over the next few hours she commented on how well mannered Emma was (*Fooled you*, Hugh thought), and Hugh heard her telling Gladys, her damsel, how nice it would be to have a companion for the girls who was young enough to be a friend to them yet old enough to provide some guidance to them. After that, events took their inevitable course, and two mornings later, their mother announced that Emma's parents had consented to allow her to come to live with the Despenser girls. Of course they had consented, Hugh thought. It was an honor to be singled out thusly by the Lady of Glamorgan, and Emma's parents, members of the local gentry, could expect that her undoubtedly modest dowry would be added to by the lady when it came time for Emma to marry. With those peculiar eyes and that tongue of hers, she would need all of the help she could get on the marriage market.

So that very same afternoon, she arrived, bringing with her a coffer containing her small wardrobe. Hugh had expected, perhaps hoped, that she would have another go at insulting him, but having made her one blunder, she spoke to him with all of the deference due to him as the Despenser heir. Soon he became as accustomed to her as he was his sisters, and as little interested in her doings as he was in theirs. In any case, he hardly saw her, for as part of his knightly training, he was usually living at court and joining it on its travels.

It was in his seventeenth year, during the Christmas of 1325, that he first saw Emma as something other than his sisters' companion. He'd not been around her in months, and those months had wrought a dramatic change in her, so dramatic that Hugh, thinking of the time he had held her close to him on his horse as they rode back to Hanley Castle, cursed himself for having made so little out of the opportunity. Emma was still tall, but she'd become slender rather than skinny, her sharp features had become interesting rather than simply stark, and she'd developed a bust. An exemplary bust, Hugh decided, contemplating it as closely as he dared, and could, under the modest robes Emma wore. So intently and unsubtly did he admire it that one of his cousins had waved a hand in front of his face, and the following morning, his father himself decided that a father-son ride was in order. Toward the end of the ride he'd said, not at all in relation to the illuminating conversation about the wool trade that they had been having, "That girl Emma has become a fine wench, but you'd best stay away, son. She can't be your wife, and your mother and sisters are too fond of her for her to become your plaything. Leave her be and let your mother find a suitable match for her."

Did his father really think he was capable of seducing her? This was flattering, at least, for as far as he could tell the attraction between them was purely one-sided. Yet he might have been tempted to disobey his father and try anyway had not Emma's mother fallen fatally ill a few months later. Emma went home to nurse her and remained there after her death to keep her widowed father company, at his request. Probably, Hugh realized later, her father had been not so much lonely as cautious; it was becoming less and less desirable to be allied with the Despenser family,

Then came the Christmas of 1326, with Hugh's father executed a month before, his grandfather two months before, and

Hugh himself under siege at Caerphilly Castle by the queen's troops. Emma's extraordinary bosom no longer mattered much. Nothing did, really, that Christmastide.

It was on a July day in 1331, the day after Hugh had been released from his captivity at Bristol Castle, the last of the various places that he'd been imprisoned, that he next encountered Emma. His mother had hastily arranged a feast to celebrate his sudden homecoming. Hugh, rather the worse for wine, had been watching from his seat of honor as the trestle tables were cleared for the dancing to begin when he saw Emma standing across the room, dressed in widow's garb. He had not known she had ever married; it was disconcerting to realize how much had happened in the four years of his imprisonment. He'd thought about her occasionally in prison, as he thought about everyone he cared for and never got to see, but as the months turned into years he'd forgotten his baser longings for her; he had even ceased to recall her features distinctly. But now that he had seen her, Hugh suddenly felt an intense ache in his groin. He rose from his seat and made his unsteady way over to her. "Emma," he said, taking her hand. "I've missed you."

"Welcome home, Hugh."

He took her arm and lurched through the nearest doorway, which fortunately happened to lead outside. "Sweet little Emma," he whispered, backing her against a wall and kissing her.

"Hugh!" Emma wrenched away and glared at him. "You are drunk."

"But I know who the prettiest lass in this castle is. Please, Emma." He tried to kiss her again but succeeded only in kissing the wall behind her as she yanked to the side. "Don't be so cruel, Emma," he complained, rubbing his sore lip. Undaunted, he put his hand on what he thought was her bosom and ended up touching her shoulder instead. He frowned in disappointment at its lack of softness.

"Hugh! You have been in prison for so long and are so far in wine that I will forgive your boorish behavior, but enough is enough. Stand back and listen to me. If I allow you to visit me tomorrow, will you leave me alone now?"

"Tomorrow," he repeated carefully, as if Emma had coined a new word.

"Yes, tomorrow. At the house my father had."

"Your father's house," agreed Hugh. "Tomorrow."

"Yes. My father's house, tomorrow. Now leave me in peace. I shall have my man take me home now."

She walked away briskly, leaving Hugh to make his meandering way inside, where in due time he was put to bed, a production that Hugh foggily recalled afterward as involving at least two of his mother's servants and perhaps his mother herself. Dim as his memory was on this particular point, it was achingly sharp when it came to his ill behavior with Emma, and late the next morning, thoroughly ashamed of himself, he rode to the manor house where Emma had lived with her widowed father. There were more ruts on the path between Hanley Castle and Emma's house than he remembered, or perhaps it was only that his horse had managed to find each of them, every one of which sent a jolt of pain through Hugh's throbbing head. Despite the difficulty of concentrating, he managed to keep the red rose he held from being crushed. "For you," he said when he was left alone with Emma. "I'm sorry I acted like such a knave."

"It's beautiful."

"But you appear to have a garden full of them, I noticed when I arrived here."

"Yours is prettier than any of mine. It's much more red, for one thing. Come. Sit and talk for a while."

Emma's house was typical of a small manor, with a kitchen, a great hall, and two private chambers, one above the other. Hugh sat uneasily in the seat Emma offered him in her own chamber. The sleeping area was curtained off from the sitting and dining area, but Hugh knew what lay behind the partition. He had never been so close to the bed of a lady, and it had been a very long time since he had made conversation with one either, except for his mother and his sisters when they had visited him in prison in his last months there. Having sat on the stool offered to him, he decided to start by elaborating his apology. "I don't know what came over me, my lady. Well, I do know; too much wine. Father told me once that I couldn't hold it all that well. But—"

"Hugh! Since when did you call me 'my lady'? Please. We have known each other too long for such formality, haven't we?" Seeing that Hugh still was at a loss for words, she added, "Is it odd, being free after so long?"

Hugh grinned in relief. "It's very odd. I awoke this morning and fretted about how I was going to get permission to go out and see you. I'd just remembered that I didn't have to do so when I heard this rustling outside, and I thought, *There's my guard, after all.* But of course it was just one of my mother's servants, coming to help me wash and dress. I'm not used to being waited on anymore, it's so strange, and I'm so awkward on a horse now, I'm surprised I made it here alive." Remembering that he had been told it was ill mannered to speak of oneself too long with a lady, he said, "I am sorry to see you have been widowed. Who was your husband?"

"Sir Alan Welles."

"Sir Alan Welles? Wasn't he in his sixties?" Emma nodded. "Emmy, why'd they marry you off to such an old man?"

She shrugged. "There was no 'they' about it, Hugh. Once your father—er—died, with my father having been in your father's service—"

"You suffered too, for his wrongdoing. Emma, I am sorry."

"It wasn't suffering, Hugh, compared to what some went through, but it was true, people stayed clear of us. My father was ailing anyway, and he died soon thereafter. I was alone then, and I thought I might as well go into a convent, even though I had no vocation. I was on the verge of doing so when Sir Alan finally spoke to me. His wife and children were long dead, and he wanted a companion to end his days with. He thought I would be good company because I had kept my father's house. I was grateful for the offer." She twisted the wedding ring on her finger. "I was a good wife to him, and he a good husband to me. He died about six months ago. I miss him." Emma swallowed hard, then smiled, though Hugh saw that her eyes were wet. "He was a respected man, though, and some of his respectability seems to have rubbed off on me, for the other tenants are quite civil to me now. One or two have been hinting at marriage with me."

"Are you considering it?"

"I don't know, Hugh."

"Why?"

She shrugged. "I suppose it just seems a little early to decide." Hugh stood. "Are you leaving so soon?"

"No. I apologize. Prison manners. I got into the habit of moving around just to pass the time, and now I get twitchy if I sit for more than a few minutes."

"Hugh, it must have been dreadful being in prison for so long. How did you bear it?"

It was his turn to shrug. "The last few months—after Mortimer was hung—weren't bad. I could go out and walk on the castle grounds, and my brother Edward was allowed to keep me company. Mother and the rest of them visited whenever they could too." He sat back down and shook his head. "Actually," he admitted, "in some ways, the last months were the worst. When Mortimer and Isabella were running the country, I never had any hope of getting out, you see. But when the king took over at last, I kept thinking every time someone came to my door, *That's the king's order releasing me.* And of course, months went by and I stayed put as if nothing had ever changed. I had just about given up ho— Why, what's the matter?"

Emma's eyes were streaming tears. "I—"

"Well, it wasn't all *that* bad. I got to take my meals in the great hall with the constable toward the end. The food wasn't bad at— Please don't cry, Emma. Christ! First I insult you last night and now I make you cry. Please, Emma. I didn't mean to make you cry."

He drew her closer to him and without quite knowing how it happened, kissed her lightly on the lips. The fervor with which she returned the kiss shocked him, and he tried again, only to assure himself that he was not mistaken. He was not. "Sweetheart," he whispered. He eased her onto his lap, still kissing her, and after a bit began to work at the fastenings of her headdress. Meeting with no resistance to the freeing of her hair, yet still not sure exactly what further liberties he would be allowed, he tentatively loosened the fastenings on the back of Emma's gown and slipped his hand underneath the fabric to cautiously lay a hand on her back, then wriggled it forward to cup a breast. Emma made no protest; to the contrary, her hands were now moving over him as eagerly as his were moving over her. Only when their mutual ardor caused the stool to tip precariously did she draw back. "Take me to your bed, Hugh."

"You mean *your* bed?"

"Don't quibble."

He picked her up, carried her through the curtain and set her on her bed, then took her into his arms once more. Hugh was by no means a virgin, but up until now he had been only with prostitutes. Mindless, brisk, and businesslike pleasure was nothing new to him, but touching and being touched with affection was. The interval that followed, as he and Emma uncovered each other's nakedness and tenderly, leisurely explored each other's bodies, was perhaps the happiest he had experienced in his young life. So moved was he that when he lay spent against Emma some time later, he was astonished to find himself almost in tears. "Thank you," he whispered.

"'Twas my pleasure." Her voice had a catch in it too.

He eased himself off her and draped his arm around her shoulders. They had been lying together in contented silence for some time when she shivered. Hugh sat up to pull the coverlet over Emma and saw when he did that there was a bit of blood on her thighs. "Your monthly course?" he asked with some distaste. Intercourse during that time was forbidden by the Church, though of course what he and Emma had just been doing was not smiled upon either, so who was he to complain? Emma shook her head. "My God! You were a virgin?"

She kissed him and pulled him back against her. "Whom better to give my maidenhead to?"

"But you were married—"

"Sir Alan was incapable, at least for this. There were ways I could please him, but this was not one of them."

"Emma, forgive—"

For an answer she kissed him again. "I have always loved you, Hugh," she said simply. "I fretted about you—secretly, of course—all the while you were in prison. I cried back there because I could not stand to think of you being unhappy. I never planned to lie with you, but now that I have I cannot regret it. I was faithful to my husband, and would still be so if he were alive, but I cannot be now that he is dead. Not with you here before me."

"What if I've got you with child?"

"Then I call him Hugh if it's a boy, what else?"

He laughed, and in due time they were making love again. Afterward, she dozed in his arms. Hugh, exhausted from the morning's activity and his dissolute evening, fell fast asleep. There was nothing in his present situation that should have caused the nightmare that had plagued him since his father's death to recur, but it did, and his scream roused Emma from her own half-sleep. "Hugh! What is the matter?"

He was so disoriented and shaking that he could not answer her for a time. Finally, he came to himself. "A dream. You must think me a weakling," he muttered.

"No, I don't think that at all. Come. Sit up and let me give you some wine. You are deathly white."

She rose from the bed, squirmed into a shift, and padded away through the curtain, barefoot. By the time she returned with a cup of wine he had recovered enough to admire the contours of her body under the shift. "What were you dreaming of?" she asked gently.

"My father." Hugh took the wine but did not sip it, instead staring off into space. "They did horrible things to him. Did you hear?" She nodded and squeezed his hand tightly. "And I dream of all of them. I thought that when I was free the nightmares would go away. I didn't have one last night."

"I doubt you would remember if you had. Hugh, they *will* get better in time. You have been free for only a short time, after all."

"I think sometimes I should have died with him, Emmy."

She wrapped her arms around him and rested her head upon his shoulder. "Hugh, you know that is not so. He did some terrible things and you did nothing."

"I should have insisted he stay at Caerphilly. Forced him, somehow. Or gone with him and faced the worst." He forced the next words out. "Sometimes I think he left me behind there to spare me. He knew they'd kill him and that if I were with him they'd probably have killed me with him."

"If that was his purpose, it was a good one. He loved you, after all. You mustn't feel guilt for his wanting to protect you."

He shrugged and took a sip or two of wine. "My mother will think I've been put back in prison. I'd best be gone." He pulled on his shirt, then turned to face her again. "Marry me, Emma."

"No, you oaf."

"Well, I've heard *that* somewhere before. But why not, for God's sake? You said you loved me."

"I do, too much to let you make a mistake like that. You must marry the daughter of a great lord like you will be."

He laughed. "A great lord! Christ! I'm not even a knight, Emmy. I've been released only on the king's sufferance, until Parliament decides what it wants to do with me. One ruffle of the royal feathers and I'm bound to find myself back in Bristol Castle."

"All the more reason you should not offend the king by marrying me. You are his kinsman, after all." Emma stared at her hands. "I would dearly like to marry you, Hugh. But it is a step you would regret in time."

He sighed. "Yes," he admitted. "Perhaps you're right." Some part of him, he knew, was relieved that she had refused. He glared at Emma anyway. "You always were irritatingly sensible, as I recall."

"More so than you, two days out of prison and asking the first woman you lie with as a free man to marry you. I *was* the first, I hope?"

"The first and the very best ever."

She smiled at him, then wrapped her arms around his neck and kissed him soundly. "Hugh, it will be a while before you find your lady, I think. In the meantime—"

"In the meantime—"

"Let us ride toward Hanley Castle together. I want to see if you are as awkward as you say. If you are, then I shall win the race we shall have."

Hugh reached for his remaining clothes and grinned. "Don't be so sure, sweetheart."

HE AND EMMA had been lovers ever since that day. Lovers— and, more important, friends. Hugh got on well with his mother and with his stepfather, who was none other than the William la Zouche who had captured his father and who had taken Hugh's surrender at Caerphilly. (His mother was not one to hold grudges.) Those younger brothers and sisters who were at home followed him about like ducklings after their mama. In those early years after his release, however, and especially in the first few months, when everybody but his own family members looked at him as they would upon a dog who might or might not bite at the least provocation, Hugh sorely needed a confidant of his own generation, and it was Emma who filled this void. During the summer and fall of 1331, he visited her at her own home, during the day, for even if he had been knavish enough to try to sneak her into Hanley Castle under his mother's nose, there would have been no place to put her. His hero-worshipping younger brothers, Gilbert and John, had begged for the honor of sharing his bedchamber when he returned from prison, and Hugh had obliged. (His Zouche brother, William, the youngest of them all, was but an infant and still preferred the company of his wet nurse.) Gilbert and John had built Hugh's single act of valor, holding Caerphilly Castle against the queen, into an epic worthy of Homer. They went to bed earlier than Hugh, of course, but when he entered the chamber and slipped under the covers, whichever brother was lying there would pop awake, snuggle close to him, and whisper something like, "Hugh, was it exciting? Were you frightened?"

"Not me," Hugh would say, lying but mindful of the needs of his small audience.

During the years of captivity that had followed his surrender (a scene that never failed to elicit groans from his brothers when Hugh told it), he had vowed to go on pilgrimage to Santiago if he was freed and pardoned. God having kept his end of the bargain (albeit somewhat tardily, in Hugh's humble opinion), Hugh kept his the following spring, first paying Emma and her bed a visit before enduring the rigors of self-enforced celibacy. It was his first time abroad, and besides the interests of foreign lands he enjoyed the anonymity of his pilgrimage, where he traveled not as Hugh le Despenser, the son of a notorious man who had died a traitor's death, but as plain Hugh, a gentleman of modest means with some knightly training. Well provided with money, and skilled enough with his sword to repel any of the rogues who preyed on those traveling the pilgrim route, he would not have been sorry to have remained wandering overseas were it not for his family and Emma expecting to see him return. So he thought, at least, until he stood aboard the deck of the ship that was taking him back home and caught his first glimpse of the English coastline, barely visible through the mist. He felt himself smile, and he smiled even more broadly when he stepped on land just in time to be greeted by a rain that was too light to make travel impossible and too hard to make travel comfortable. In Spain the sun had shone every day, and now that Hugh thought about it, that was simply unnatural.

Back in England, having first hurried to Hanley to spend a joyous afternoon in Emma's bedchamber, he moved onto the manors that the king had granted him as a form of recompense for his father's and grandfather's much more extensive estates, all of which had been forfeited to the crown. Running them, and helping his mother with her own estates, someday destined to be Hugh's provided that he stayed on the king's good side, kept him busy. Still, though nothing he was doing was bringing the name of Despenser into ill repute, nothing was giving it any new luster either. Fortunately, the Scots soon remedied this situation.

Hugh rode off to his first battle in the summer of 1333 with mixed feelings. He had a certain liking for the Scots. Briefly during the second Edward's reign, he and a couple of other youths had been hostages in Scotland. He had been treated well by his hosts, and his short stay there had passed pleasantly. Besides, like his mother, he held to the principle that no one who had sent Mortimer home in humiliation, as England's old enemies had in 1327, could be completely without merit. Too, it was humiliating to be riding in the retinue of his cousin Edward de Bohun as a mere man-at-arms when the Bohuns and all of Hugh's other male relations had been knights, or even knight bannerets, for years. Yet when battle was joined at a place called Halidon Hill, Hugh's ambivalence and shame deserted him and he fought fiercely, sharing in an English victory that no one had seen in a generation.

Knowing that he had fought well, Hugh was nonetheless somewhat wary when Bohun rounded up him and a couple of others to see the king. Even after he arrived in the king's presence and realized that he had been brought there not to be reprimanded but to be knighted, he was a bit uneasy when Edward's sword thumped upon his shoulder, lest the king decide to strike off a Despenser head out of sheer habit. But nothing went amiss, and his royal cousin stared at him thoughtfully after Hugh obeyed his command to rise. "I have been told that you are a good fighter, *Sir* Hugh," he said. "You shall be useful to me, I think."

Hugh looked around the field, where England's enemies lay dead in heaps. "Provided the Scots can keep on obliging," he said dryly.

"Oh, they will," said the king. "You can't keep them down. Count on it." He clapped Hugh on the back a bit awkwardly; he had witnessed the deaths of both Hugh's father and grandfather, and Hugh often wondered what he had thought about the experience. It was a question he would never ask, though. "Good work," the king concluded.

The king had been right that day; the Scots continued to keep the English busy. Hugh spent much of the next few years fighting in Scotland. Gradually he came to be trusted by his fellow men; he saved their skins a time or two and had his saved in re turn. His brother Edward married and had a son; his brother Gilbert became a squire in the king's household. The king granted Hugh a bit more land.

Eleanor, his mother, encouraged by this improvement in the family's fortunes, had begun urging Hugh to marry, subtly at first, less so as the years went by. Was it Hugh's comparative lack of land that was holding him back? Surely he could find a heiress to remedy this, and perhaps the king would allow Eleanor to grant some of her land to him now that Hugh had proven his loyalty. Was it that no one wanted their daughter to marry him? That could not be so; he was handsome and brave and destined to be Lord of Glamorgan! Was it that he did not want to be married? But that was his duty! Why, his younger brother had married before him! This last thread of her argument was unanswerable as far as Eleanor was concerned, and she never missed a chance to bring it up, especially after Edward's wife bore her first son. When was Hugh planning on begetting his own legitimate heir?

Hugh fended off this questioning (it would have been called nagging had Eleanor been of less exalted bloodline) as deftly as he could. After his aborted attempt to marry Emma, he had not proposed to anyone else, suitable or otherwise; he sensed, as his more isolated mother perhaps did not, that there was still a certain wariness toward him. Moreover, he had inherited his share of the family pride; though passion had made him propose to Emma, in a cooler moment, when he was ruled by his head and not by his groin, he realized that he should marry a woman of his own rank. A rich merchant's daughter would not do; neither would an ordinary knight's. She would have to be a great lord's daughter, as Emma had said. In the meantime—and it was probably his main reason for staying single—he was more than content with Emma. Sometimes he visited her at her own home; sometimes she traveled to one of his own manors. Hugh often wondered whether word of their affair had reached his mother's ears, for though he and Emma did not flaunt their relationship, they had occasionally been spotted on their horseback rides together. It was a subject, however, on which his lady mother remained silent.

The king, meanwhile, was beginning to turn his attention away from the Scots and toward France. Recognizing the importance of a vigorous young nobility who supported his war efforts, at the Parliament in the spring of 1337 he created seven men earls, most of them the men who had been with him that night in 1330 when Roger Mortimer was surprised and taken prisoner. Hugh, of course, heard this from a distance, for no Despenser had sat in Parliament since 1326. He held no grudge against William de Montacute, the new Earl of Salisbury, or his kinsman William de Bohun, the new Earl of Northampton, or most of the other new earls. Had they not helped the king overthrow Mortimer, Hugh knew, he himself might still be in prison or dead by now. No, what rankled Hugh was the naming of Hugh d'Audley, his uncle by marriage, to the earldom of Gloucester, an earldom held by Hugh's own grandfather Gilbert de Clare. It was Hugh le Despenser who was the late Gilbert de Clare's eldest grandson, and he could not help but feel slighted and resentful that Audley, married to a Clare but not of Clare blood, should have the earldom. Six years had passed since Hugh le Despenser's release from prison, and the luster of those early tokens of royal favor, his manors and his knighthood, had long since faded. He was a knight with two hundred marks of income a year, so were many other men. Was it so wrong to covet what his kinsmen had: high standing, wealth, a place in

Parliament? Was he no better than his father, who had coveted so much? Worried, he took the question to his confessor, who reminded him sternly to heed his father's ill fate and to keep his mind focused on the next world instead of being led astray by the vanities of earthly titles and wealth.

Well, this was easy for his confessor, not a young man, to say. But at age twenty-nine, Hugh had another thirty or even more years in this world, if he were lucky. It was a long time to keep one's mind focused on the next.

His mother, newly widowed from Lord Zouche and seething with resentment herself at the slight to her son in favor of her sister's husband, was too partial to be a good confidant. Hugh, therefore, took his troubles to Emma, as ever. "Perhaps he would have given you the earldom of Gloucester if your mother had been gone and you the Lord of Glamorgan, Hugh," she said gently as they walked together one afternoon. "Audley was a wealthy man already. You told me that the king had to grant land to some of the other earls to support their new dignity."

"Perhaps he would have," said Hugh. "I wouldn't have it at that price, Emmy; I love my mother. She's been through so much and I want her to be happy. But I've slogged around Scotland for four years now at the beck and call of the king, and it's brought England little and me nothing but a knighthood and an intimate knowledge of those damn oatmeal cakes of theirs." He absently touched his finger to a battle scar on his thigh. "Maybe I should go abroad after all; there's bound to be discord somewhere."

"Hugh! I was frightened that you'd never come back after your pilgrimage."

"I might not have if it weren't for you," Hugh admitted. He sighed. "I'm no more than a mercenary now anyway. I'm not fighting for England; I'm not fighting the Scots; I'm fighting for myself." He flushed, about to speak a thought he had not previously ventured to put into words. "I think sometimes that my life was spared for a purpose, Emma. The purpose of bringing honor back to my family name. It was a honored one in my great-grandfather's time. You've heard of that Hugh? The one who died fighting for Simon de Montfort."

"I've heard of him."

"He's been written about by some of the chroniclers," said Hugh. He had had copies made for himself, though he had never been much of a reader, and lugged them with him from manor to manor so that he could read them in the privacy of his chamber when he was so inclined. In truth, though, he no longer had to read the passages in question, for he'd memorized them years before. "Montfort told him to flee and save himself while there was still time, and he refused. He said, 'My lord, my lord, let it be. Today we shall all drink from one cup, just as we have in the past.'" Hugh recited the last words self-consciously. "That is how I would like to be remembered. Not as the no-account son of a sodomite and an extortionist."

"Hugh! I remember your father. He was more than that. He was—"

"A pirate as well."

"He did no worse than many lords would have in his position. And you of no account! Hugh, you have let this business with Audley affect you too much. The king does not regard you in that light, I am certain."

Emma and Hugh were having this conversation near his southernmost manor, Thorley on the Isle of Wight, not far from Yarmouth. Normally Hugh rather enjoyed the feeling that he was at the very edge of the kingdom, especially when Emma visited him and they could stroll hand in hand by the sea as they had been doing, but in his present mood he wondered if the king might have had reasons of policy for giving him such a remote manor. He was getting ready to propose retiring to his chamber for a consolatory session of lovemaking when he saw one of his men hurrying toward him. "Sir Hugh? A message for you from the king."

Hugh read the letter he was given. "Speak of the devil—not to use the term disrespectfully. The king has summoned me to him to discuss a matter of business."

Traveling by water from his lodgings to Westminster a few days later, Hugh flinched as he saw London Bridge, which until the end of 1330 had been adorned by his father's head. From those who had been in London at the time he knew the exact spike where it had been displayed, though it like the rest of his father had long since been moved to Tewkesbury Abbey. Even without such an association, he could take little pleasure in a journey to London. It had been the Londoners who had rioted against his father and the second Edward, killing several people, and it had been the Londoners who almost more than anyone in England had gleefully welcomed the invasion of Isabella and Mortimer, though they'd lost their enthusiasm for the ruling pair soon enough. Still, it having been several years since he had last been in the city, Hugh found himself looking around with interest as the boat in which he sat made its way down the Thames. He began to wish he had brought Emma along to see the sights.

Inside Westminster, he followed a servant to the inner chamber where he was to meet the king. He hardly needed the guidance. As a page to the second Edward and the eldest son of his favorite, Hugh had had the run of the place in his day, and old memories began to return as he retraced a journey he'd so often taken as a youth. Probably there were passageways he knew about that the man leading him did not; Hugh saw him miss at least one very handy shortcut Hugh had often utilized.

Edward was waiting for him, rather to Hugh's disappointment, for he had recognized the window seat in the chamber as one in which he'd carved his own name years before and had hoped for some time alone so that he could see if it was still there. "Your grace."

"Sir Hugh. I was saddened to hear of your stepfather's death."

"Thank you. He was a good man. I shall miss him, and my mother is very grieved about it."

"Yes, they seemed happy together." The king cleared his throat. "My brother spoke well of you."

Hugh inclined his head gratefully. His recent service in Scotland had been with the king's brother, John, Earl of Cornwall. Hugh had genuinely liked the twenty-year-old earl, and it had helped that John had pleasant memories of Hugh's mother, who'd been in charge of his household for a time. Yet Hugh had also frankly hoped that his service with the earl might lead to some preferment, perhaps at last the chance to command his own men, and John had foiled those hopes by dying of a fever a few months before. Sincerely as Hugh had mourned his young kinsman, he could not help but think John might have been considerate enough to hold out a little longer. "I was grieved to hear of his death."

"Come, Sir Hugh, we're kinsmen. Let's speak less formally. I know you've heard about the earldom of Gloucester. You can't be pleased about it."

"It is not for me to say to whom you give titles, your grace," said Hugh distantly. Edward made an impatient gesture, and Hugh added, "No, I am not. I know full well you could not give me an earldom even if you wanted to; it would be too awkward after all that's happened. Perhaps it'd do me more harm than good in the long run by arousing old grudges against my family. And I don't pretend to have distinguished myself enough to have earned one anyway. But the earldom of Gloucester does have meaning for my mother, and my own son might have aspired to it. But that's all gone now that it's in Audley's line."

"Son? You're not even married." The king squinted at Hugh. "Why haven't you married?"

Hugh decided not to tell the king that he sounded eerily like Hugh's own mother. "I suppose I have never been tempted."

"No one has ever proposed a match for you?"

"No one but my mother, and hers have been only theoretical."

"You've never proposed one yourself?"

"Not in some years."

"The lady was unwilling?"

"The lady was wise."

"I see." For a moment, Hugh thought the king was going to inquire further; Eleanor certainly would have wished him to do so. Instead, he shrugged and ran a hand through his hair, a reminder to Hugh how young he still was. "Well, what's done is done as far as Gloucester and Audley are concerned, but it's not our intention to leave other deserving men out in the cold. The manors you have now are held only until your mother's lands come to you, aren't they?"

The king knew the answer to that as well as Hugh did, but Hugh answered anyway, "Yes."

"As a mark of our favor toward you, we shall grant them to you in fee simple. And we shall grant you others as well. You'll have Chittlehampton and Langtree in Devon, Rotherfield in Sussex, and the reversions of others once Edward de Bohun's widow dies. And some woods, knight's fees, and advowsons as well. Our men will give you the details. All in all, it'll probably double your income."

Hugh bowed and thanked the king. What was Edward up to? Hugh was not naïve enough to suppose that the king was acting out of any great solicitude for his Despenser kinsman's feelings. With this French business the king could use all of the support he could muster; he could ill afford to have militarily able men, even outsiders like Hugh, sulking idly on their estates. So he was being thrown a bone.

But a tasty one it was, for his income could certainly use amplification. Hugh could not stop himself from smiling. Then he recalled what he had been brooding upon on the trip to London. "Your grace, there is something else I would ask for."

The king frowned.

"Not more land, your grace. Not a title. Just this: I would like to lead men in battle. I'm capable of it, I know. You yourself said that your brother praised me, and he wasn't one to give it when it was undeserved. I can win men's respect; even now there are men from Glamorgan and from my own manors who would fight with me. I've already pledged to serve under my kinsman Warwick in this Scottish business, and I shan't renege on that promise, but later—" Hugh looked down at his shoes. "It would be the greatest gift you could make to our family, your grace, to let us regain your trust by that means."

Edward said, "Very well. We'll let you prove yourself."

"You won't regret it." Hugh relaxed. "Your grace, do you mind if I look at the window seat?"

Edward stared at him, probably wondering if his relation's mind had been addled by this sudden improvement in his fortunes. "No."

Hugh walked to the window seat and stared down at it. There, carved awkwardly in the wood—his handwriting had never been a marvel—he saw his name. "Still there," he said to himself softly. He smiled again.

HUGH HAD LAST SEEN HIS MOTHER deeply mourning the loss of her second husband, but otherwise in apparent good health, so he was shocked at the change he saw in her when he returned to Hanley Castle. Eleanor's face was gray and pinched with pain, her brilliant red hair had become almost colorless at the roots, and she hobbled when she could move around at all. She had some female ailment, the physicians told Hugh, that had crept up on her slowly and about which nothing could be done.

On the last day of June 1337 she died, surrounded by her children. As she drew her last breath, having spent most of the previous night and the morning drifting in and out of consciousness, her children sought comfort from each other: little Lizzie clutching her oldest sister Isabel's hand; the girls who had been made nuns praying together; Gilbert pretending not to need the hand his brother Edward shyly placed on his shoulder. William and John, the youngest two boys, turned to Hugh. He put an arm around each of them and stayed silent while six-year-old William cried and while eleven-year-old John endeavored not to. After a while had passed, he said, "You are very tired, both of you, and so am I. I want you to have something to eat and then to rest. I need to ride to clear my head. Then I'll come back and you shall share my chamber tonight. Just like you used to do. Would you like that?"

They nodded and dutifully left the room. Seeing that ten-year-old Lizzie was being consoled by Isabel and that the rest were bearing up as well as could be expected, Hugh stood. He was so tired from his vigil by his mother's deathbed that he felt lightheaded, but he needed fresh air more than sleep. As he made his way out of Hanley Castle, he noted that all the servants, even those with whom he had been on the most informal terms, were suddenly treating him with extreme deference. He could not put his hand on a door without having one or sometimes two people spring ahead of him and hold it, and someone must have guessed intuitively that he would want to ride, for no sooner did he ask for a horse than his favorite palfrey stood saddled before him. Any remark any of them made to him was prefaced by "my lord."

The ride to Emma's was a short one, but he took it slowly because of his fatigue. Word of his mother's death had reached her household before Hugh did, for the servants' faces were somber, and they bowed deeply to Hugh when he rode up. Emma herself, when she came out to greet him, had put on black robes. "My lord," she said, and curtseyed.

"Not you too," he protested, and kissed her cheek. "Will you go for a ride with me?"

She nodded, and soon they were seated together in a secluded spot on a hill where on other fine summer days they had often brought a meal, ate it off a blanket they spread, and then kissed to their heart's content. Today, however, there was nothing but talk between them. "I've wished so often to come into my inheritance, Emma. But I didn't know what I was wishing for! She was only forty-four, you know. I'd give anything to have her back now. I feel so guilty."

"All heirs dream of getting their land, Hugh, I think. You have no cause for guilt. And you were a good son to her. I visited her a time or two while you were away, and I asked if there was something I could do to help her. She always said no, that you had made sure she had all she wanted or needed."

"Little enough."

"Enough to make her content and at ease, as much as she could be, poor lady. It was a mercy she did not linger; she was in dreadful pain sometimes, Hugh, in places where she would probably not tell a man. She was a brave lady."

"Yes," said Hugh, and crossed himself, as did Emma. He stood and looked at the valley below him, dotted with fat sheep. They were his sheep now, as was everything he could see. And over in Wales lay Glamorgan, the acquisition of which had enriched and destroyed his father in a few short years. Now it too had become his. It was both a tragedy and a marvel, he thought, how the ceasing of a human heartbeat could change so much in so short a time. "Lord of Glamorgan, Emma, whether I like it or not. Do you think I'll be a good lord?"

"The best," she said, and patted his cheek. Hugh retained her hand for a minute, then brought it to his lips. "I'd best get back to my castle," he said.

THE NEXT FEW MONTHS passed in a flurry of firsts. His first expedition to Scotland as a banneret, his first summons to Parliament. Hugh had not entirely expected the latter, having half assumed that as a Despenser his chief duty in Parliament would have been to stay a hundred miles away from it. Yet the summons came nonetheless, and as no self-respecting lord could come to Westminster without a full contingent of followers, he was trailed by a dozen men when he rode into the city.

Emma came with him too. With William being educated at Glastonbury, Lizzie boarding with the nuns at Wix, and John serving as a page in the queen's household, Hugh's own household was empty of brothers and sisters. Emma had begun to live openly with him, though nominally she had her own chamber to which to retire at night. Hugh's confessor had shaken his head at this sin on his master's part, but he contented himself with the reflection that now that Hugh had come into his lands, he would surely marry someday and that a marriage on Emma's part would duly follow. It was lucky, the confessor often thought, that no bastard had resulted from the affair.

His fortunes having changed since his last visit to London, when Hugh had stayed at a cramped inn, Hugh had leased a handsome house, overlooking the Thames, for his stays in the city. It was a large house for a single man to rattle around in, and after consideration he had asked Emma to join him there. By doing so, he knew, he was in effect proclaiming her his official mistress, for although she had traveled with him before, it was only between his own estates, where none but the locals paid attention to their lord's comings and goings and to the question of with whom he came and went. Now, as he would be visited by some of the friends he had gradually acquired over the years of fighting side by side with them, Emma could not remain hidden away. Besides, he was proud of her. With her unusual but striking looks and the elegant robes and handsome jewels Hugh had insisted on presenting her with when he came into his inheritance, she was the match of any countess. If only he could marry her! But as dearly as he loved her, he was at heart a realist, and he knew that such a marriage would do nothing to bolster his improving fortunes.

One Parliament followed another. All during this time, the English and the French had been tweaking each other's noses, daring the other to begin a war, and in the summer of 1340, near the harbor at Sluys, each side got a taste of what was to mark the next hundred years to come. Hugh, master of his own ship now, would never forget those hours in the English Channel. Men fought hand to hand, the decks on which they stood slippery with blood and rocking madly from side to side. From another ship, a group of English ladies, brought to stay with Queen Philippa in Flanders, watched in terror as men toppled into the sea, some dead, some dying, some frantically hoping to escape. When it was over, though, it was the English who were able to make the joke that if the fish in the sea could speak, it would be French that came out of their mouths.

The king took a nasty wound on the thigh and spent some days recuperating on the cog *Thomas*, where Hugh was rowed over to join him one evening. After wishes for the king's speedy healing had been expressed and some business matters had been discussed, Edward said, "I've been considering your marriage, Sir Hugh."

"My marriage?"

"About time you thought of it yourself, isn't it? Now, see here. William de Montacute has a daughter. Several, as a matter of fact, but the girl in question is thirteen or so, I believe. A marriageable girl; indeed, she's a little widow. High time she married again. A good alliance for you. She's not an heiress, of course, but she'll bring her dower from her Badlesmere marriage, which is ample, very ample. Montacute will like the idea too, once he gets out of France." William de Montacute, the Earl of Salisbury, had been a prisoner there for several months. "They're not in a position to argue with a reasonable ransom now that the sea is full of Frenchmen, so I think he'll be home soon. He'll like it, I daresay, making his little girl Lady of Glamorgan. So what of it, Despenser? Why not marry the Montacute girl? Oh, and she's a pretty little thing, I've heard, so you needn't concern yourself on that score."

Hugh stood open-mouthed. Marriage to an earl's daughter, and that earl the king's closest confidant? He could hope for no better a match, he knew. Only a fool would say no to such a proposition, even if it had not come from the king himself. And yet at that moment, he could think of nothing but Emma. For nine years they had been all in all to each other.

Yet it was she herself who had left him free for such a match on that July day when they had first come together in her bed. He gulped and knelt. "I would be honored to marry the young lady, your grace."

AFTER HUGH AWOKE from his nightmare, he tried to obey Emma's advice by going back to sleep. Instead, he lay there, listening to her breathing beside him and reflecting that it would be the last time they lay together. It had been nearly a year since his conversation with the king, but all was at last settled. William de Montacute had been released from captivity and had given his consent to the marriage, after which the Pope had duly granted Hugh le Despenser and Elizabeth de Montacute a dispensation to marry. So later that morning, Hugh would be setting off to Tewkesbury to await his bride.

Emma would be going back to her own home. Though there had been nothing meretricious about her relationship with Hugh, he had nonetheless given her many gifts over the years, and the possessions that she had accumulated in the chamber that had become known as hers had taken longer to pack than either she or Hugh had anticipated. Watching her worldly goods being placed by his servants into their coffers and loaded onto a cart, Hugh had realized that there would soon be no sign in Hanley Castle, or any of his other residences, that Emma had ever lived there. His only keepsake from her was a ring that she had given him a couple of years before. Hugh wore it on the same hand as a ring that had belonged to his father, his one tangible reminder of the man other than his tomb at Tewkesbury Abbey, and as he watched the rings glisten side by side, he wondered if Emma might as well be just as dead to him.

But she was stirring next to him, and he reached for her and held her close to him until she fully awoke. "Hugh, you hadn't had your bad dream for years until just now. Is something troubling you?"

"Only you leaving. That's enough, I suppose."

"Hugh, I must leave. I am no—"

"I know. You're no adulteress, and I'm not a knave, as much as I wish at the moment we could be both. Christ, I'll miss you, though."

Parting upon his marriage to Bess had been a mutual decision, though Hugh knew only too well that he could have been talked out of the notion had Emma been less principled. But she had said, "I love you, Hugh, but I will not lie with a married man, even one whose wife is too young to be a full wife to him just yet. We must part now and live the rest of our lives as friends only."

"Friends only," Hugh had agreed, and his new chaplain, William Beste, had heartily approved when a less enthusiastic Hugh told him of the plan. Infidelity, he had reminded Hugh, had been the first of his father's great sins, and it was one Hugh should strive in particular to avoid. "But he was unfaithful with the old king. So what I just avoid our king's bed?" Hugh had suggested. "I wouldn't have a problem there at all. Neither would the king, I'm sure."

Beste, whom Hugh had chosen for other virtues instead of a sense of humor, had merely shaken his head.

Emma said, "I will miss you too, Hugh. But we have been separated before, when you have gone off to fight. It will be hard, but I will get used to it."

"You can think of this as a very long fight, perhaps?" Hugh smiled in spite of himself. "Emma, I wish you'd consider this. Let me find a husband for you. Someone who will be good to you, who will protect you. Someone not liable to drop dead next week, perhaps. Someone such as Sir—"

"You would pass me to someone else?"

"Good Lord, no, not like that! But it will be lonely for you, and I thought that with—"

"No, Hugh le Despenser!"

Emma never called him "Hugh le Despenser" except when she was irritated with him. Hugh obediently subsided. Then Emma broke the silence herself. "I know you meant well, Hugh."

"I did, Emmy, truly. I thought only that otherwise you might be tempted too, and with a husband—"

"I have a stronger will than you realize, Hugh, after all of these years. But yes, perhaps, one day I may be able to contemplate getting married to someone else. But it is not a step I can take now. You are not that easily replaced, for one thing." She sighed. "I do wish we had had a child together, though."

"I do too, now," Hugh admitted. In the early days of their relationship, after their first few heedless couplings, he had fretted over the possibility of getting Emma with child. He had gone so far as to try to withdraw himself from her just in time, but she had not allowed it. "I want your child, Hugh," she'd whispered. "Please." Hugh, despite some misgivings, had acquiesced, as there was no danger, after all, that their child would go hungry; he or she could marry respectably or find a congenial spot in the Church. It appeared, though, that all of his misgivings had been for naught, for in all their years together, Emma had never missed a monthly course, only been late a time or two. Emma had decided that her barrenness was a punishment for her sin, though Hugh had been secretly relieved. His own mother had borne him and nine other healthy babes safely, but not all women were so lucky, and it would have been a terrible burden had Emma died giving birth to his child.

He thought of suggesting to Emma that she might be blessed with issue were she properly married, but wisely decided against doing so. Instead, Emma said abruptly, "What is your bride like, Hugh? You've said little about her except that she's the Earl of Salisbury's daughter and almost fourteen."

"Bess, as she hates me to call her? A bit spoiled by Papa Montacute, it would appear, and not at all pleased with the idea of having a Despenser for a husband, if I'm not mistaken. She's a pert little thing. When she's displeased with something I say, which so far has been quite often, she wrinkles her little nose, like this." Hugh's own nose was not one that easily wrinkled, but he demonstrated as best he could. "It's quite fetching, actually."

"You sound half in love with her already."

"I could be, I suppose. Whether she comes to like me is another story altogether."

"Of course she will, Hugh."

He shrugged and reached for her again, but it turned out that neither of them, on this last possible occasion for them to make love to each other, was truly interested in doing so. Instead, they lay in bed holding each other for a while, then dressed and saw to the details of their day's business; Hugh to that of trying to forget his misery, Emma to that of moving her last things out of Hanley Castle. By mid-morning all of her goods were packed and headed in a cart toward her house. Then it was Emma's turn to leave also. She and Hugh walked silently out to where Emma's horse, a present from Hugh, had been saddled for her. Emma's own manservant stood well away as Hugh stepped up to help her onto her palfrey. "I know you can take care of yourself, you always have," he said. "But you know you can always turn to me if you need assistance. Me, or any of my household."

"I know, Hugh."

"I love you." He swung her up on the horse.

She bent and kissed him on the forehead. "I love you, Hugh."

He watched as she rode away, traveling the same path that he had ridden to her house on that summer's day nearly ten years before. Around him, men were coming in from the fields for their dinner, men were loading things in carts to be transported to his manor at Tewkesbury, men were waiting to see him with business and petitions. Yet as Hugh stood there in the midst of all of them, on the eve of his marriage, he had never felt more alone in his life.

3

June 1341

In between last-minute fittings of Bess's wedding apparel, the Countess of Salisbury was taking the opportunity to give Bess some womanly, and motherly, advice. She had begun with the subject of the Marital Act, which as Bess understood it from her mother was something that could be reasonably enjoyable to women but which was something that men could not bear to be without. Hugh, it seemed, would be no exception to this rule. "Men are not faithful by nature, though many are," Katharine told Bess. "You must accept it if Hugh strays occasionally. And at his age, and with you not being of a condition to lie with him just yet, you must expect that he will have known women before, and may continue to do so after your wedding. As long as he does not flaunt them in front of you, you must bear this patiently."

"What if he *does* flaunt them in front of me? Can I get the Pope to annul our marriage?" Bess had happy visions, all of a sudden, of Hugh bringing a stable of whores to dine at table with him and of a suitably furious Pope tearing their marriage contract in two. She could almost hear the satisfying rip the parchment made.

"I doubt he would do so," said Katharine most unhelpfully. "Hugh is a decent man, after all, and not a fool. I've no doubt that he will treat you with all due respect."

Bess scowled. A worrisome thought came to her then. "Mama, does Papa stray?"

"Certainly not, and it would be a sorry day for him if he did," said Katharine.

Leaving Bess to puzzle over this inconsistency with the advice she had just been given, Katharine turned her attention to the casket of jewels sitting nearby. They had been brought to Bess the day before, an early wedding present from Hugh. Philippa, Sybil, and Agnes, Bess's younger sisters, had been goggle-eyed when they were taken out, and Bess herself had been impressed, though she'd tried to not seem so. "Have you decided what ones to wear yet?"

"I hadn't thought of it. I thought to wear just the ones that Papa gave me."

"And offend Hugh? Besides, child, they are magnificent." She opened the casket and lifted a ruby brooch in one hand and a sapphire bracelet in the other. "His mother's, I suppose, and some of them perhaps his grandmother Joan of Acre's. The first Edward's daughter, you know." Katharine held the ruby brooch up against Bess's wedding dress. "It will go beautifully with it."

"Do you think Hugh's mother wore them upon her marriage to Hugh's father?" Bess shuddered.

"Quite possibly; the settings look old enough. Now, don't you get it into your head not to wear them because of that! It is not every girl who gets to wear jewels like these on her wedding day—or ever. They're too fine to let sit in their casket because of your superstition."

Holding the brooch herself, Bess had to agree.

The Montacute family was already in Tewkesbury, where Hugh had a manor close to the abbey founded by his mother's ancestors. Though the manor house was a good-sized one, nearly as large as a small castle, it could hold only the bride and groom and their immediate families and servants, even with most of the servants bedding down in the great hall. With the wedding to take place in two days, the house was quickly filling up, as were the local inns. Anyone with a respectable home who could drag

in an extra bed or pallet to accommodate a paying guest was doing so, and a small forest of pavilions was sprouting nearby as
well. The taverns were full, and their keepers, in the highest of
spirits, were heard to say that they wished the lord of the manor
got married every year.

With each new arrival from Hugh's family who arrived at
Tewkesbury manor over the next day and a half, Bess's head
swam like the fish embroidered on her new bed coverlet. Hugh's
four sisters were the first to appear. The eldest was Isabel, the
Countess of Arundel. Bess already knew not to expect her to be
accompanied by the Earl of Arundel. The couple had married as
children and had disliked each other from the start, and the cir-
cumstance of their fathers being executed a week apart by
Mortimer and Isabella, though it might have brought some couples closer together, had not improved their marital relations.
They had lived together just long enough to have a fourteen-
year-old son, Edmund, who came with his mother to his uncle's
wedding.

"No need to be formal," said Isabel briskly as Bess acknowledged her sister-in-law's higher rank with a curtsey. "I am a
countess for now, but I shan't be as soon as Richard finds a
higher class of woman than the doxies he usually runs with and
gets the annulment he is always threatening me with. Oh, it's
true, Edmund, don't blush. But here! See what I have brought
you as a wedding gift! Oh, there's the usual gold cup that you'll
receive later, but I thought you might prefer this."

A page who had been standing in the background stepped
forward and solemnly placed a ten-week-old puppy into Bess's
arms. "The best of my finest bitch's new litter," Isabel said.
"Hugh said that yours had died a few months ago, and I thought
you might like this one."

Bess had indeed mentioned in passing to Hugh that she was
fond of dogs and that her old one had died recently, but it was
something that she hardly thought he would have remembered.
She cuddled the pup as it licked her nose. "'Tis so kind of you,
Countess."

"Isabel."

Isabel was giving Bess a detailed account of her dog-breeding, and Edmund had struck up an animated conversation with Bess's younger sister Sybil, when a girl of about fourteen rode up, followed by a waiting woman, a few men, and a very scruffy-looking, mud-splattered boy of about eleven. "My youngest sister, who's married into the Berkeley family," said Isabel. "She is an Elizabeth like you, but she is Lizzie to us, and as I suppose you shall be Bess to us, that will save a great deal of trouble. Lizzie! This is Hugh's betrothed, Lady Bess."

Elizabeth de Berkeley smiled at Bess as the boy, evidently a Berkeley page, awkwardly assisted her from her horse. Though quite womanly looking, with a full bosom and a nicely rounded rump, Lizzie still wore her curly brown hair flowing, as befitted only maidens and new brides. Was Lizzie still deemed too young to bed with her husband, wherever he might be? "Will your lord be coming?" Bess asked, realizing when it was too late to retract her question that this might be another situation like that of the Arundels.

Lizzie pointed to the boy. "My husband is right here," she said resignedly. "Maurice will never go around a body of water if it is shallow enough to ride through."

"Cools off the horses. And if I had gone the long way I wouldn't be here yet."

"*I* took the long way and arrived here at the same time as you," said Lizzie.

"Because I waited for you, slowpoke."

"And you have gotten yourself all dirty for Lady Bess! For shame, Maurice."

Maurice smiled and bowed to Bess, then pointed to his wife. "She acts proper now," he said in the tone of one making a great confidence, "but she can play at football nearly as good as a lad, I'll tell you."

Lizzie rolled her eyes. "Do clean up, please, Maurice. Lady Bess will think us savages."

"They'll be fine breeders when they reach the age," Isabel prophesized as Hugh's servants arrived to take the new arrivals to their chambers.

No sooner had the Countess of Arundel and Elizabeth de Berkeley been accommodated than Joan and Nora le Despenser arrived. They and a third sister, now dead, had been forced by Queen Isabella to take the veil only weeks after their father's death, Isabel escaping the queen's net because of her marriage and Lizzie escaping because she was still in her mother's womb at the time. Bess's heart ached for those young nuns who had never had a vocation and who had been denied the chance of grand weddings for their own selves, but Joan and Nora did not seem inclined to self-pity. They ran into their brother's arms as soon as they were assisted off their horses. "I thought you would never marry!" said Joan as Hugh embraced her.

"One would think you were the one who had taken vows!" added Nora.

Presently Hugh's youngest Despenser brothers, Gilbert and John, and his Zouche half-brother, William, arrived. Bess had barely learned their names and gotten a sense of their dispositions—Gilbert was boisterous, John reserved, and William studious, she decided—when a commotion was heard at the entrance of the great hall in which dinner was being served. Hugh, his soldier's instincts taking over, half rose from his seat, then relaxed as two small boys barged into the hall and ran toward the high table, heedless of anyone or anything blocking their path. "Uncle Hugh!" they yelled.

"Boys? But if you are here, your father must—" Hugh stopped as a man, smaller and with more delicate features than Hugh but clearly his younger brother, entered the hall more sedately but nearly as eagerly as his sons. "You came!"

"I wasn't sure I should, but Anne insisted. She said she felt fine and that I shouldn't miss your wedding."

"True, it was rather ill-bred of the girl to catch a cold right before her brother-in-law married. I'm glad you came, Edward." Hugh embraced his brother and then turned toward Bess. "My lady, this is Edward, and these two ruffians"—he waved a hand toward the boys, who had been caught by the hands by a stout nurse who had puffed in after Edward—"are his sons. His eldest two sons, for his third was born just the year before. His lady is incapable of breeding anything but boys, it seems. The younger is named Thomas and the older is another Edward, I'm afraid, but as they'll ignore you when you call anyway, it shouldn't be a source of confusion."

"Come now, they aren't that ill-behaved," Edward protested. He turned to Bess with an apologetic look. "Truly, my lady, they are not, but they had to ride in a litter for a very long ways, and when it was opened—"

"They found their way to freedom," Isabel put in. She gave her younger brother a kiss on the cheek. "You spoil them, Edward, always have."

"Perhaps," Edward conceded. He blushed.

His shyness appealed to Bess, who said, "I am sure they are good boys. There is nothing more wearisome than riding in a litter on a fine day like this."

Edward beamed at her, and Bess knew she had made a friend for life.

The Despensers bantering amongst themselves and making themselves agreeable to their eldest brother's chosen wife, the dinner passed pleasantly for Bess. But after dinner there was more trying-on to do, the tailor having been busy with Bess's wedding dress during the meal, and a crisis presented itself when the ruby brooch Hugh had given Bess could not be found. When Bess's puppy was seen wearing a look of indigestion, this gave rise to the direst of suspicions, which were alleviated only when the brooch was found under a pillow. The puppy, however, was far from having its name cleared, for further investigation turned up Bess's bridal slippers, which bore unmistakable chew marks. In the pandemonium of scolding and barking that followed, Bess's wedding nerves shattered. She threw herself on her bed, sobbing, and lay like that until Katharine cleared the room.

"There is time to fix the slippers, my dear. And if not, no one will notice them."

"I don't *want* to marry, Mama. Please don't make me. There are so many girls he could marry—can't he find someone else?"

Katharine held her as she cried a little more. "Child, it is only your nerves that are torn to shreds. You have been meeting so many people, and sitting through that long dinner, it is no wonder. You need some air. Why don't you go ride a bit?"

The prospect of a ride was tempting, especially as going to the stables would give her a chance to look at the snow-white palfrey that Bess had seen being led into a stall rather furtively the day before. When Bess admired it, the grooms had been maddeningly vague about to whom it belonged, which had led Bess to suspect that it was yet another wedding gift from Hugh. But a horse would have to be made ready and saddled, and in the interim her sisters or her prospective sisters-in-law might well take the notion to join her. "I'll walk to the town instead."

Accompanied by the requisite page, Bess soon arrived in the thriving town that had grown up around Hugh's manor. But peace was as elusive there as it had been in the manor house. The street was full of people who had come to see her married, traveling to and from their lodgings and the manor house. As Bess's page was wearing Montacute livery, there was no escaping identification as the bride-elect. Stranger after stranger stopped to pay his respects, until Bess thought she would scream. Only one place appeared to be tranquil: the Abbey of St. Mary the Virgin, or Tewkesbury Abbey as all called it, where she was to be married the next morning. "Let us go in there," she hissed.

A monk, elderly and slow moving, greeted her as she stepped through the heavy wooden door leading inside the abbey. "My lady?"

Evidently the old monk was shortsighted, for he was one of the few people in Tewkesbury who did not recognize the livery of Bess's father. "I am Elizabeth de Montacute."

"Ah, yes. Our lord's bride," the monk said in such a reverent tone that Bess was momentarily taken aback before she realized that he was referring not to the deity but to Hugh.

From his outstretched hand, Bess guessed that he was intending to show her around the abbey. More company, the last thing she wanted. Pretending not to have heard him, she broke away and hurried into the choir, muttering a prayer of repentance for her rudeness. Left in peace, for her page had stayed behind with her would-be host, she slowed her pace and looked up, then gasped at the beauty and intricacy of the vaulting above her head. Ribs, painted with gilt, joined each other to form floral patterns, colored in brilliant blues and reds. Light shone into the choir from seven stained-glass windows. The window on the far east represented the Last Judgment, the damned being hustled off to hell by an avenging angel as a kneeling, nude lady, who Bess later learned represented Hugh's mother, looked on. The four adjacent windows had been given over to biblical kings and prophets. As Bess turned to the last two windows, her gaze was met by those of a host of stained-glass knights, their coats of arms identifying most as ancestors of Hugh's mother, Eleanor de Clare. Hugh's own notorious father, resplendent in a surcoat marked with the Despenser arms, stared down coolly, daring anyone to question his fitness to stand beside so many great men.

"Do you like it, my lady?"

Bess whipped round and saw Hugh standing beside her. "What are you doing here?" she asked, realizing too late the impertinence of her question, for if there was one person in Tewkesbury not a monk who had the right to be in the abbey, it was surely Hugh.

Hugh seemed unoffended, however. "I came here to pray for the souls of my parents. The monks do so regularly, of course, but I'm inclined to think that my father could still use some more help."

"Oh."

"Well? What do you think?"

"It is beautiful," Bess admitted. "Did you commission this work?"

"No. I am seeing through what my father began and what my mother continued after his death. Should you like to see their tombs, my lady?"

Bess did not, but she nodded and allowed Hugh to take her arm and lead her to a chest-like tomb, its many niches occupied by figures of Christ, the Apostles, and a host of saints. In a recess within the tomb lay the effigy of Hugh's father, dressed in the same manner as his stained-glass counterpart and looking on the whole to be quite pleased with his beautiful surroundings. Bess was half curious to know whether any of his quartered remains had been salvaged, but it was hardly a question she could ask his son. Then Hugh to her surprise said dryly, "In case you are wondering—most people do, I'm sure—he is all here, within reason of course. The men who had the task of reassembling him, so to speak, were rewarded very well by my mother."

"I should think so," said Bess lamely.

Hugh crossed himself, and Bess tactfully moved a distance off while her husband knelt and prayed for a short time. He caught up with her as she was heading toward the Lady Chapel. "My mother and stepfather are in here, Lady Bess. There's my mother's tomb here."

A lady's effigy gazed up at an intricately carved canopy. Hugh's mother lay with hands clasped in prayer, as had her first husband. Though the effigy wore the headdress that no respectable lady would be seen without, even in death, the sculptor had left some stone hair, painted in a red as vivid as the colors of the lady's robes, visible. "My mother asked that her tomb resemble that of her uncle, the second King Edward. She was very fond of him, poor man."

"It is very fine. But why didn't she ask to be buried with your father? Did he ill-treat her?"

"No. He loved her and he was a good husband, save for—" Hugh shrugged. "They loved each other very much. But she loved my stepfather too, and in the end she did not want to choose to lie near one over the other. She fretted about it a good deal toward the end of her life, poor thing." Hugh half smiled. "To ease her mind, I finally told her that I would place her at an equal distance between their tombs, and so you see I did."

"Do you miss him?" Bess asked daringly.

"Every day." He tapped Bess on the nose. "You're wrinkling it in disapproval, I see, but I too loved him. He was the only father I had, after all, though I did get on well with Lord Zouche."

"Are you like him?"

"No. He was much more clever." He smiled at Bess. "Sweetheart, I know it can't be easy, marrying into a family with a reputation such as mine has, but there is nothing to fear, from me or from my father's ghost, I assure you. Will you let me show you that I can be a good man and a good husband to you?"

Taken aback by his frankness, she nodded. Hugh bent and kissed her lightly on the lips, so quickly that she was in doubt a moment later as to whether the kiss had taken place. "I have not asked you why you are here, Bess."

"I needed to be away for a while. The wedding preparations—"

Hugh laughed. "Poor Bess. My robes have been ready for weeks now, and all I have to do tomorrow is put them on and get on my best horse. It's different for a bride, isn't it? If you came here for peace, then, I shall leave. You have a man with you, I assume, to take you home?"

Home. The word jarred, though in less than a day, Tewkesbury manor would indeed be her home. "Yes."

"Good day to you, then." He kissed her hand this time and turned away. Soon Bess could hear him conversing with someone, probably the monk who had greeted her. Left alone at last, she was at a loss for what to do. As she was in the chapel, it seemed most natural that she pray, but except for her first husband, whom she'd barely known, she had no dead to pray for, or at least none whom she had known more than fleetingly. Nor could she in good conscience pray that something prevent her wedding the next day, not in the chapel built by Hugh's own family. She would have liked to have prayed that she have a noticeable bosom on her wedding day, like Joan of Kent's, but not only did this seem somewhat frivolous, it would take more of a miracle at this late date than the Lord was perhaps willing or even able to provide. Flummoxed, she finally prayed that her wedding day would be a sunny one and that her slippers could be mended.

Both these small prayers, it turned out, were answered, though this heavenly benevolence made Bess's wedding morning no less a nervous one for her. As she was assisted onto her new white palfrey, which wore a spanking-new saddle that was bejeweled almost as finely as Bess herself, she was certain that she would fall off, exposing her legs and God only knew what else to Hugh's household, all of whom were standing around watching her as if they had never seen a girl getting married before. She would be the laughingstock of Tewkesbury for years to come. She stayed on, however, and also managed to avoid sitting on her thick, dark hair, which she normally wore in a single braid but which on her wedding day fell unbound to her hips.

The palfrey flicked its beribboned tail as two of her father's youngest and most handsome pages led Bess slowly toward Tewkesbury Abbey, followed by a horde of wedding guests. Bess was relieved that the recent birth of a son to Queen Philippa had kept the king from putting in an appearance, although if he had it would have given the people standing alongside the well-worn path to the abbey something to stare at besides the bride. There were plenty of them standing there, for aside from the frantic cooking for the wedding feast to be held later that day, only the most essential work of the manor was being done. Everyone, even those too lowly to attend the wedding mass, had been invited to the feast.

A woman cackled to her companion, "Pretty little chick, but not ready for our lord to bed, I'll wager!" Bess, whose mouth had been fixed into a smile, forgot herself and glared daggers at the woman. She sat up straighter and thrust her chest forward a bit, trying to create the illusion of a bosom.

Hugh had already arrived at the abbey door when Bess appeared. As he was merely the groom, and a familiar sight in Tewkesbury, his progress had not excited much interest beyond a few cheers, though he had been followed by a half dozen knights and cut an impressive figure in his new robes, which nicely set off his auburn hair and beard, dark brown eyes, and lean body. He smiled at Bess as she was assisted off her horse and led by her father to stand at Hugh's left side. "You're lovely," he said, so softly that no one but the immediate bystanders could hear.

Bess listened as Hugh's chaplain, William Beste, asked the bystanders if they knew of any reason why she and Hugh should not be joined together in matrimony. No one obliged her by saying yes. As the chaplain dutifully recited the terms of the dispensation the couple had received, Bess, looking at the chaplain without seeing him, began to consider whether she would have to keep her hair covered from now on. She'd not covered hers after her first marriage, as there could have been no pretense that she was anything but a virgin, but now that she was old enough to bed Hugh in theory if not in fact, she would probably be expected to conceal it. This was a pity, she thought, as her hair had always been considered her greatest beauty. Perhaps—

"I will," Hugh said firmly.

Bess jumped as Beste began asking her if she would obey, serve, love, honor, and keep Hugh. Weakly, she agreed with that, and everything else that was asked of her, until Hugh's small nephews, conscripted into the ceremony at the last minute, swaggered up with a pillow on which lay a gold ring set with sapphires. Hugh took the ring, and little Edward and little Thomas beamed as the chaplain blessed it. Evidently, the most important part of the ceremony had been accomplished, in their eyes at least.

"With this ring I thee wed," Hugh said, and smiled again at Bess. He slid the ring onto her finger. Bess felt the tears sting at her eyes. There would be more blessings to follow, and a mass to be said inside the abbey, but she was now irrevocably Lady Despenser.

Hours later, the wedding and the wedding feast over, Bess and Hugh knelt by the bed that was to be hers while Hugh's chaplain blessed it. As it was known that she and Hugh would not yet be sharing a bed, she did not have to put up with the indignity of being put into bed with him while the guests made bawdy jokes. Instead, the crowd quietly departed, followed by Hugh himself.

Her maid had undressed her and was drawing the bed curtains when a knock sounded. "Me, Bess."

"Hugh?" Though Bess was wearing a shift, she drew the covers up to her chin as if she were stark naked. "You are not—"

"I've not come to bed you, sweetheart. But it seemed odd to leave you on our wedding night without a private word or two." He grinned. "And I wanted to check on your feet. I trod on them several times while dancing."

"They are fine."

"I never was much of a dancer. Perhaps you will improve me." Hugh sat down on the bed. Bess had heard tales of grooms who became so drunk on their wedding night that they were barely conscious come bedtime, but Hugh had drank sparingly, a point Bess had to concede in his favor, especially since a number of the guests had not been so prudent and had been staggering about during the blessing of the bed. "Do you think it went well?"

"Did you think it would not?"

He shrugged. "I was worried a bit. Some of the people there tonight hadn't spoken to anyone in my family for years. My aunt Margaret, for instance, and her husband the Earl of Gloucester."

"The tipsy lady?"

Hugh grinned. "Aye. I confess I had my men fill her cup more often than necessary, to see if it would mellow her a bit. It worked; I actually got a smile from her at the end of the evening, did you see? But it could have had the opposite effect, so that was luck in itself. And I was worried about my aunt Aline—the older lady in black you saw—because she has hardly spoken to anyone outside our family for years. I thought she would be miserable, but my brother Gilbert had her dancing! So everyone seemed to get along, that I could tell. Do you think so?"

Realizing that Hugh was anxious for her opinion softened Bess a bit. "Yes, Hugh."

"I'm glad." Hugh yawned. "You must be tired, sweetheart, and so am I, I confess. I won't keep you up any longer. But would you let me hold you while you fall asleep? It will help us get used to each other."

Too tired to argue, Bess nodded. Hugh slid onto the bed, not getting under the covers, and lay next to her. The night had turned chilly, and to her surprise Bess found herself enjoying the warmth of her husband's body next to hers as she closed her eyes and waited for sleep. As her thoughts began to tumble against each other, she dreamily remembered her mother's talk of the day before. "Where will you spend the night?" she asked, only half aware of what she was saying. "With your mistress?"

She could not see her husband's face suddenly change, and was too near sleep to notice the awkward pause before he spoke. "No, sweetheart. *You* are my mistress." Hugh kissed her on the cheek. "Good night, Bess."

"Good night," Bess mumbled.

4

August 1341 to July 1342

Although Bess had not yet warmed to being Lady Despenser, she soon came to enjoy being Lady of Glamorgan. While she was used to being treated with deference, especially since her father had gained his earldom, she naturally had always been overshadowed by her parents. Riding side by side with Hugh and being greeted by his tenants as their new lady as he and Bess traveled through his estates with his retainers in tow was a far different thing from riding behind her parents, lost in the midst of their entourage, or staying in the children's chambers at some far-flung castle while her parents went to court.

Just as pleasurable was the novelty of having large sums to spend on herself. Bess had been stunned when she saw the amount Hugh had allocated to her, and even more stunned when she realized that provided that she did not overspend or neglect her almsgiving, Hugh would not question her as to what she did with it. Her parents had always been generous to her, but having her mother order that new robes be made for her at suitable times was very different from having her own ample household allowance to spend as she liked, with no interference from anyone. Bess was not extravagant, and she was careful to follow her mother's example and set aside a generous sum to be used for the needy, but as that still left her plenty of money for her own feminine wants, she had been quick to order herself an extensive wardrobe. Hugh was the sort of man who dressed in whatever his servants chose for him each morning, and all of his robes, though costly, looked fairly much alike in color and pattern, but he made a visible, if often unsuccessful, effort to notice and admire whenever Bess sported a new gown.

Bess's time was not occupied solely with such frivolities. Hugh's tenants went to him with their serious disputes and when justice had to be done, but soon it was to Bess they came when their babies were ailing or when a good word from their lady might clear the way for a betrothal or soothe a minor disagreement. Her mother's training, supplemented by that of Elizabeth de Burgh, had prepared Bess better for this than she thought, and she was pleased to see tangible results when a child felt better after taking some of the herbal remedies Bess had prepared or when two quarreling women went off in harmony. Hugh had also been only too glad to hand over the domestic details, such as planning of meals and the ordering of livery, to Bess, so she stayed busy and content after the excitement of the wedding festivities died off.

She had no complaints about Hugh. Although he came to her chamber each evening to kiss her good-night, he never touched her more intimately, and their relationship in most respects was more like that of brother and sister than husband and wife. Hugh's own affairs kept him busy, but he was careful to spend some time alone with Bess each day, usually on horseback, for Hugh's imprisonment had left him with a distaste for sitting indoors for long periods, and riding gave Bess a chance to become familiar with his estates. He'd also given Bess one of his own prize falcons, and though Bess was not as keen on the sport as her husband, she was sensible of the value of the gift and made an effort to take an interest in it.

For the times when Hugh was gone, she had the company of her damsels. Though she had been accompanied to her marriage by her old nurse, Mary, it had been understood that she would want more youthful companions and that for the sake of goodwill they should be chosen from families that had ties to Hugh.

Bess was introduced to many young women as she and Hugh traveled through his estates after their marriage, but she had been slow in finding suitable candidates. A girl younger than she would be a nuisance, while one slightly older might tend to be patronizing and well enough developed to set Bess off at a disadvantage. A lady too much older would be little better than another mother, and Bess, though she loved her mother dearly, was rather enjoying not being under her watchful eye. A lady of Bess's own age could not impart the womanly wisdom Bess at times desired. A lady about Hugh's age or a little younger would be ideal, but most such ladies she encountered were married, bound to their own husband and children and not likely to be companions for more than sporadic periods.

Then the tenants around Hanley Castle came to pay their respects, and Bess met the widowed Lady Welles. Bess liked her immediately and invited her to visit the next day. Her impression of Emma only improved as the women sat making garments for the poor and chatting about the neighborhood. Lady Welles's manners were neither too formal nor too familiar; she laughed when Bess's puppy propelled itself into her lap; and she told Bess just what she needed to know about the other tenants without being malicious or mealy-mouthed.

The very next day, Bess sought out Hugh. "I wish to invite one of your tenants to be one of my damsels, Hugh. The young widow who visited here yesterday. Lady Welles."

"Lady Welles?"

Bess had never seen her husband look so peculiar. Was he offended by her choice of Lady Welles? It was true that Bess had questioned some of Hugh's household about Emma, but had gotten the vaguest of answers. Finally, Hugh's laundress, when pressed, had acknowledged that Lady Welles tended to keep herself to herself, and for that reason might be regarded as a "little strange." But she attended the village church at Hanley punctiliously, the laundress hastened to add, and was entirely respectable.

Now Bess said, "Yes, Hugh, Lady Welles. Don't you think her suitable?" It occurred to her that Hugh with all of his traveling might not know some of his tenants more than superficially. Unconsciously, she lifted one of her puppy's paws for emphasis. "You do know whom I mean, don't you?"

"Yes, I know her." His expression did not change.

"Well? Is there something against her character?"

"You mistake me, sweetheart. I think no ill of Lady Welles; quite the contrary. I have known her—that is, I know her—for a good woman. But she has been widowed for many years, and is very used to living by herself and running her own household. I am not sure she would adapt well to being at someone's beck and call, even yours. But you can certainly ask her if you wish. Just don't be put out if she refuses graciously."

"Oh, but she would not refuse! I have asked her already. She said she would be happy to join me here, if you consented. And now I am asking for your consent. Please, Hugh?"

Hugh hesitated and finally said, "Very well. I will have my steward speak to her about finding her someone suitable to watch over her estates for her while she is away. She'll need someone reliable and trustworthy."

"Thank you, Hugh." Bess leaned over and kissed her husband on the cheek, the first time that she had done so, though the effect was a little spoiled when she followed the kiss up with one on her puppy's head. She hurried off, eager to relay the good news to Lady Welles.

"ARE YOU MAD? What were you thinking?"

Emma, assisted by her maidservant, was packing clothing into a coffer. "It was your lady wife's idea, not mine. How could I have offended her by refusing, Hugh?"

"You could have lied to her. Told her that you were prone to fits of melancholy madness, I don't know. Told her that you were in the earliest stages of leprosy. Told her something, for God's sake. You're clever."

"I like your lady wife. She's a charming young girl, and I was pleased that she thought of me. She would have been suspicious, perhaps, if I had refused. It is an honor few widows in my position would turn down, after all."

"Other widows weren't my lover for nearly ten years, Emma."

Emma shrugged. "I shall enjoy her company, more perhaps than you realize. It is lonelier here now than I thought it would be." She ducked low over the coffer she was filling.

"If you'd marry as I have suggested, you wouldn't be lonely."

"Now you sound like your own mother."

"Who was a sensible woman most of the time. Come. Let me find a good man for you."

"I found one, Hugh. I do not wish to find another so soon." She straightened. "You could have ended the business by withholding your consent."

"With her staring at me with those big brown eyes of hers? And that puppy Isabel gave her staring at me too? I was outnumbered." Hugh recalled the kiss she had given him and could not help but smile. Had she given him one at the outset, he would have found it difficult to hold out as long as he had. "Anyway, it's something on which she has her heart set. I would have to tell her the truth, and I would just as soon not. She likes you very much, and she was happy when I told her yes."

"Then we must resign ourselves to this, mustn't we? Don't fear, Hugh. We shall be safe together; after all, there's no reason for us to ever be alone with each other." She sighed. "It is true that I have had my temptations now and then, but I master them."

"It's me mastering mine that I'm worried about."

"You want her to be happy. You will not hurt her. I know you better than that."

"Beste will probably think I've brought you in for my own debauched purposes."

"He shall keep you in line too, Hugh. And soon your eyes will have no reason to stray. Your lady wife is a pretty little thing, and she is losing that coltish appearance girls of that age have and getting a shape to her."

"I've noticed," Hugh admitted. "Just as *you* got a shape," he muttered.

Lady Welles joined the Despenser household the next day. Hugh's chaplain had indeed shaken his head over the arrangement, but Hugh and Emma gave him no basis for complaint. As Emma had predicted, they were never alone with each other, though as Hugh's household traveled in and through Wales during that summer and fall, they were often only a horse's breadth apart, the horse in question being that of Bess, who rode happily in between the former lovers, smiling occasionally at her husband and chatting animatedly to Lady Welles. So fond had Bess become of Emma, in fact, that Hugh found himself feeling a bit jealous of her at times. Coming to say good night to Bess of an evening, Hugh would as often as not find them lying on Bess's bed chatting together while Bess's old nurse, Mary, who was increasingly afflicted with pains in her joints, sat smiling benevolently at them from her perch on a stool by the fire. "What on earth do you ladies find to chat about all the time?" he asked when he found them in a particularly giggly mood one evening at Cardiff Castle, a locale that always put Hugh in a somewhat subdued mood anyway. The Despenser party had arrived there just that afternoon, and Bess and Emma had been no less animated on the ferry ride over.

"Your lady wife was imitating poor William Beste, my lord," said Emma, who never failed to greet Hugh formally.

"I'm so sorry," sputtered Bess. "But he is quite pompous."

"Well, show me your art," said Hugh.

Bess pulled a long face and said, "Repent, my lord and lady. Repent."

Her imitation was so good that Hugh would have been hard-pressed to explain it away had the unfortunate Beste himself appeared at that moment. He snorted with laughter before adding, "He's a good man."

"Good night, my lady." Emma slid off the bed and drew Bess's bed curtains as Mary rose stiffly to her feet and made a feint at assisting her. "Good night, my lord."

"Good night." Hugh settled next to Bess in the space that was still warm from Emma's body. Bess stiffened slightly, as she always did, then relaxed with a visible effort. Hugh knew that she was never was at ease with him alone as much as she was with her ladies present. But she was trying; Hugh had to give her credit for that. After a moment or two she said brightly, "This is a pretty castle, Hugh."

"Yes, it's one of my favorites," he lied.

"I like being able to see the water."

"Yes, so do I. We'll ride alongside it tomorrow if you like."

She nodded. He leaned over to give her his good-night kiss, wondering as he did so whether she was as acutely aware as he was of her blossoming womanhood. The boyish figure she'd had when they first became betrothed was rapidly disappearing, as Emma had noted, and the fine, light fabric of her shift might have been designed as an instrument of torture, so tantalizingly did it hint at the new Bess underneath. Remembering his promise to Bess's father that he would not bed her for a year, Hugh distracted his thoughts from the natural direction they were taking by picturing Alice his laundress, whom Hugh had taken into his service after his release and who was now close to sixty, in his bride's place. It was an act of conjuring that was steadily growing more difficult, but he managed it once more, for now. "Good night, sweetheart."

"Good night, Hugh." She smiled at him, as she always did, and with a yawn of contentment rolled on her side, stretching her pretty, long legs after that day's long travel. Probably, Hugh thought morosely, the year of chastity could not pass too slowly for her taste.

Hugh had only a couple of more months to consider the developing charms of Bess and the attendant frustrations, however, for the Scots had been about their old business of raiding England, and King Edward decided that it was time to put it to a stop. In October he began to move north, and Hugh was among those lords summoned to join him. He obeyed with some reluctance, for it seemed a pity to leave his little bride all by herself in his large castles, which Hugh knew well could be lonely places, even with her ladies and most of his household present. He was relieved, then, to hear just before he departed that Joan of Kent, Bess's sister-in-law, had invited her to visit for a while, and that his own sister-in-law Anne le Despenser would also welcome a visit from his new bride.

Bess bade her husband a warm, if not heartfelt, farewell. She had come to like him but not to love him, and she was certain that he could take care of himself in battle and would be coming home safely. He always had, after all.

When she arrived in North Wales at Mold Castle, which her brother Will and Joan had been granted by the Earl of Salisbury, Bess was chagrined to find that her friend was looking more beautiful than ever. Bess had not been unmindful of her own maturing and improving looks, and she had noticed Hugh's eyes traveling toward her body on more than one occasion. Though she knew she could never approach Joan in beauty, she had at least hoped, therefore, that the contrast between them had become less sharp. But as Bess had been maturing and improving, so had Joan, and the distance between them in terms of appearance was as wide as ever.

Life, Bess reflected, was deeply unfair. The more so, she thought after she had been in Joan's company for a day or two, in that Joan did not appear to appreciate her good fortune. She was distant, as she had been at her wedding and at Bess's own, and half of the time she scarcely seemed to be listening to what Bess was saying. "I don't know why you asked me here," Bess said after a day or so of having to repeat herself so often that one might have thought Joan was hard of hearing. "You can't be bothered to attend to me."

"I am sorry. I have not been a good hostess, I know."

That was strange too, this meekness. Joan, like all of the king's close relations, was possessed of a temper; Bess had felt it on more than one occasion. Perhaps she was ill, Bess thought for the first time. "You are not quite well, perhaps?"

"I am fine."

"How do you get on with my brother?"

"Why do you ask? Do you think I am not a good wife to him?"

This, sharply spoken, was more like the Joan whom Bess knew, but as Bess had not meant her words to carry any sting, she was flummoxed as to how to continue. After a moment she said, "Of course, I think you are a good wife, Joan. I meant no harm."

Joan shrugged. "Do you like Hugh?"

"He is kind to me and very good-natured."

"Have you lain with him yet?"

"No. My father told him he had to wait a year." Believing that she could hardly ask Joan whether she had lain with Will, Bess remained silent.

"I have lain with my husband," Joan announced at last.

"What is it like—with a man, I mean?" She hastened to add, "Not with Will in particular."

"It hurts the first time, and then you ache the next day. Dreadfully, like falling off a horse. Will was nervous the first time and had too much to drink. I didn't like it."

"Do you now?"

Another shrug. "It's all right. Perhaps I shall get with child soon. Then perhaps—"

She started sobbing, quietly at first and violently, so violently that Bess shoved open the chamber door and screamed for assistance. Joan's attendants raced inside, followed by Bess's, but all were shoved aside by Joan's nurse, who like Bess's had stayed with her old charge to tend her as a bride. "It's all right, my lady. Come. Let's put you to bed." Gesturing toward the others to stand aside, she helped Joan to her feet and led her toward the inner chamber where Joan and Will slept. Soon she returned alone. "My lady is sleeping. Let us go elsewhere."

"Matilda, what ails her?" Bess asked. "Joan has never been sickly in the past."

Matilda shook her head. "I don't know, Lady Despenser."

Bess was jolted by the use of her married name. "Has she seen a physician? Does my brother know? I am sure he would be most concerned if—"

"She just needs her rest, my lady. It is a—female thing."

Bess was inclined to remind Matilda that she too was a female, but recognizing the futility of pressing the matter further, she obediently left the room. She hoped to garner some more information later from Joan herself, but she was never alone with her thereafter. In any case, Joan was cheerful throughout the rest of Bess's stay, and extremely affectionate toward Will, so Bess convinced herself that there was no cause for concern. Perhaps, she guessed, Joan had been hoping to have conceived a child by now and was upset that she had failed; she might have even had a miscarriage. Had Will perhaps been overbearing? Irritating as Joan could be to Bess, she was still fond of her and wished her well, so she determined to speak to her brother. Her opportunity did not come until the day before she was to leave for her visit to Anne le Despenser. "Will, I hope you don't expect Joan to get herself with child right away. She is but young. Mama told me that it can take several years sometimes."

"I don't. Whatever gave you that idea?"

"Joan was act—"

"One of her spells? Oh, she has them from time to time, you must have caught her in one. She says it's when she has her monthly courses."

That made perfect sense to Bess, who herself was irritable and moody at that time. "I see."

"Women are strange," said Will cheerfully.

Satisfied that she had done what she could for Will and Joan, Bess then traveled to Essendine in Rutlandshire, where Edward and Anne le Despenser had their principal residence. Edward and his squires had gone to Scotland with Hugh, leaving Anne at Essendine Castle with her three small sons. She hated it, she confided to Bess within five minutes of her arrival, when Edward was gone, and if she had things her own way, the English would live in eternal peace so that she would never be parted from him. "But it is his obligation as a knight to fight, he tells me, and I know it is," Anne said apologetically. "But I wish he was not so conscientious about attending to his duties! He doesn't like it much, I know; he would much rather be here with me and our boys, attending to our lands here. Don't you wish Hugh was home, Bess?"

"Indeed," said Bess a little awkwardly, for in truth she had not given Hugh much thought, though she dutifully included him in her prayers each night and certainly wished him the best.

"I thought that Hugh would never marry. We never could figure out whether he was just being particular, or whether he just liked being a single man, or whether people were just shying away from him because of his poor father. You know about his father, I daresay?" Bess nodded. "It was horrid, wasn't it? My Edward says very little about him, but I know he loved him dearly, and I am sure Hugh did too. Your husband Hugh, I mean. It is so cruel for men to use men so— Edward! Don't pull the dog's ears, or I shall pull yours, young man. Now, where was I? Oh, Hugh's marrying. I regret having missed the wedding, but I had the most dreadful cold, and my little Hugh was teething as well. Edward told me that it was very grand and that you were a beautiful bride. He must have liked you very much, for he even told me what you were wearing, and normally he doesn't notice things like that. You must have made quite an impression on him."

Anne took a deep breath and sipped from a cup of wine. "People do say I talk a lot," she said apologetically.

Bess widened her eyes in surprise.

"Oh, they do, and I suppose they're right. Edward just listens; he's such a darling. We liked each other the moment we met, and then Edward asked my brother for his permission to marry me, wasn't that sweet? Much more nice, I think, than having everything arranged beforehand. Of course, your marriage was arranged, and nothing wrong with that; mine would have been if Edward hadn't sought shelter at Groby during a dreadful rainstorm and met me. I am so glad he did before they married me to someone not nearly as good and kind. Wasn't that providential? But I am being rude, chattering on like this about Edward and myself. Tell me about yourself."

Bess could hardly equal Anne's conversation, but she told her sister-in-law about her family, then finished up by telling her about her travels through Hugh's estates. Having summed up her fourteen years on earth in a few minutes, she asked Anne about her boys, knowing that her hostess would be unable to resist such a topic. It was one near at hand, for Edward and Thomas had been running in and out of their mother's chamber throughout the conversation, and little Hugh had just been taken out by his nurse for a nap. "They are fine boys," Bess said. She did not have to stretch the truth, for all three looked vigorous and sturdy for their ages.

"Yes, we have been blessed, haven't we?" Anne looked suddenly guilt-stricken. She lowered her voice and said, "In truth, sometimes I wish for the next one to be a girl. I am so outnumbered here! But they are good boys, when they are not savages."

"It is odd to think that I may have one—years from now, I mean," Bess hastened to add, fearing that Anne might misconstrue her words.

"Well as you are one of how many—five, did you say, no, six?—and Hugh was one of ten, I think your chances will be excellent on both sides!" Anne smiled at the smock she was making for her son Hugh. "We are sisters, so you will not be offended if I ask if you are bedding with him yet?"

"I am not—offended or bedding with him. My parents wanted us to wait a year."

"Well, I daresay you will like it when you do. Hugh is a deal older than you, but he will be gentle about it, if he is anything like Edward."

A loud and intense dispute between Anne's eldest boys having erupted in their nearby chamber, Anne excused herself. As the sounds of her reprimands and the boys' self-justifications echoed down the hall, Lady Welles, who had been chatting quietly with Anne's damsel as the sisters-in-law got acquainted, said, "My lady, my head aches dreadfully. I would like to lie down in our chamber, if you can spare me."

"Goodness, Emma! Please do, poor thing. I am sorry you have been sitting here in pain all of this time."

"It just came on, my lady. I have had them before. It will pass when I have been in the dark and quiet for a while."

"Then do lie down," said Bess. She rose and kissed Emma on the cheek. "Feel better, my dear."

Anne returned, flushed from battle. "You shall not see *them* again today, my lady; they are being punished for their silly bickering with no supper tonight." Behind her back, Anne's lady smiled, and Bess, who suspected that some food would find its way to the boys' chamber, perhaps through Anne herself, tried hard to suppress her own smile. "I passed Lady Welles. Is she ill? She looked peaked."

"She has a headache, but she said it will pass with rest."

"Poor dear, if it does not I will summon my physician immediately. A pity she is a widow still, I wonder that she has not remarried. She must have loved her husband deeply, I suppose. If Ed—" Anne crossed herself. "I could not even bear to think of that. I hate it that he has to fight. Stupid Scots! But we were talking of Hugh. You know, when I married Edward, I was so foolish when I realized that I was not his first woman, I cried! It was silly of me, I know now; for goodness' sake, he was a grown man! But I had lived in Groby all of my days and had very little idea of what men get up to, of course. I trust you will have more sense than I about those things when the time comes. Hugh is in his thirties, after all, and men do get around a bit."

"My mother said that he might have had a mistress, that men often did."

"Oh, he might well have. Indeed, I think Edward even mentioned her once. Not by name, but I do remember he talked of Hugh and his lady friend going to Glamorgan. But that was a couple of years ago. And when we visited there was no one but family staying with Hugh."

"Oh," said Bess. She wondered, a little jealously, what this lady friend had looked like. Russet-haired like Joan of Kent, dazzlingly blond, or a black-haired beauty? Surely a man as wealthy as Hugh would have had a good-looking mistress. She wondered how she compared, with her rather serious face and her hair that would never be any shade but plain brown. "He never described her?"

"No. Hugh didn't flaunt her about, I suppose." Anne looked a little guilty. "I am sure she is long gone by now," she said apologetically.

Bess stabbed at the embroidery in her hand with a sudden irritation.

BY LATE JANUARY 1342, Hugh had returned home, none the worse for wear, for little had happened on the Scottish campaign, to the king's frustration and to Anne le Despenser's relief. Bess herself was pleased enough to have Hugh back, and they settled back into their brother-sister relationship quickly and pleasantly, at least from Bess's point of view.

The talk among Hugh and his knights in the great hall was now of Brittany, as it had been for months. The Duke of Brittany had died last April, survived by a niece, Jeanne de Penthievre, and his half-brother, John de Montfort. Jeanne had married the Count of Blois; John the redoubtable Joan of Flanders. Bess, though she was not all that interested at first in the talk going on around her, soon became aware that France supported the claim of Blois, King Philip's nephew, while Montfort had appealed to the English king for his aid. By the time the English returned from Scotland, it was Joan, the Countess of Montfort, who was leading her own cause, for John de Montfort had gone to Paris to negotiate and ended up as Philip's prisoner.

Edward determined to come to the countess's aid. By March, he had sent a force, under the command of Walter Mauny, to assist her, though it was not until May when his troops arrived. With the English-French treaty under which Edward had been laboring set to expire, more forces were to come, and everyone knew that in the end it would not be the countess pitted against Blois, but England pitted against the might of France.

Hugh received the expected message from the king in the summer; he was to sail from Dartmouth to Gascony, where his men would aid in diverting the French from Brittany. In preparation for his departure, Hugh, accompanied by Bess, traveled to his manor of Ashley, not far from Winchester, awaiting the arrival of his soldiers.

Bess helped with the preparations as best she could, and by the time all of the men had arrived at Ashley, from where they were scheduled to leave for Dartmouth the next day, she was tired and eager to be left alone for the evening. But the men had to be fed, and it being perhaps the last time they would see comfortable quarters for quite a while, they had to be fed and entertained in style that last night at Ashley. When after a long evening Hugh came in to her chamber for his nightly visit, Bess prayed silently it would be a short one. She smiled at Hugh as he parted the bed curtains and sat down next to her. "I shall miss you, Hugh," she said politely. "I hope this business won't take long."

"Who knows?" Hugh shrugged a bit too elaborately. Though he was by no means drunk, he was slightly tipsy, Bess thought; the wine had flowed particularly generously in the manor's great hall that night. Bess herself had had a little more than to which she was accustomed, but the effect had been only to give her a headache in addition to fatigue. "It could be weeks. Could be months." Hugh toyed with a pillow for a moment or two, then looked into Bess's face. "Sweetheart," he said. "We've been married for over a year."

"Yes, Hugh." Her heart began to pound.

"We may not see each other for months, Bess. We may not see each other ever again, you know. It's always a possibility. Do you understand, Bess? It's time we became man and wife, truly."

"Hugh—"

"I won't hurt you." He took her in his arms, then gently eased her backward onto her pillows. "I promise, sweetheart."

He seemed to believe that the discussion was over, for his hands were exploring under her shift. But Bess was not ready to acquiesce. She tried to push him off her, but he was far stronger than she. "Hugh! I—I am not ready yet. I am—"

"Nonsense," said Hugh, whose lips were roving now. He stopped for air and smiled. "Haven't you seen yourself lately? You've grown up, Bess."

"Please, Hugh!"

He shook his head and began to push the shift up toward her waist, not roughly but insistently. "My love," he whispered. "It'll be fine. I promise."

Bess felt not fear but anger, anger that he was paying no attention to her wishes. She pounded on his back and hissed, "You are only a bully, Hugh! No better than your father!"

Hugh pulled away instantly and got off the bed. His face was ashen. Then he said quietly, "I will not trouble you anymore, my lady. Good night."

She lay motionless for a while after she heard her chamber door close behind Hugh. There was no sound from Mary or Emma; probably they had guessed what was in her husband's mind and had made themselves scarce. She sat up, rearranged her shift, and closed the bed curtains herself. Then she lay back beneath the covers. It was a warm night, but she was shivering.

What had she done? It was a husband's right to take his wife when he wanted, Bess knew full well, and Hugh had been waiting patiently enough for well over a year. He had spoken truly; her figure was no longer that of a child. With Ashley packed full of Hugh's men, she had seen glances sent her way when she moved about that had left her in no doubt of that, even if she had not had the additional evidence of the fabulously expensive mirror Hugh had bought her as a belated New Year's gift.

And Hugh had not been brutish about the affair. Bess had seen women whose husbands were cruel to them, women with bruises on their faces even while they were big with child. Hugh, she was well aware, despised the husbands of such women; once in Bess's presence he had taken aside a tenant of his whose wife had appeared with a purple welt on her face and had spelled out to him, in no uncertain terms, what would happen to him at Hugh's own hands if his wife displayed such bruises in the future. The man had taken heed. Hugh was not this sort of man; his hands had been ardent just now, but not rough.

She might not see him for months, as he had said, might not see him again. Hugh had told her once about the battle of Sluys, one in which so many men had drowned. More than once, he'd said, he had thought he would not come out of it alive. What if the sea crossing turned into another Sluys, one where the battle went to the French this time? What if Hugh met his death in Gascony?

He had wanted so little from her, really. A night with his wife to think back upon in the weeks to come. And she had not only spurned him but hurt him deeply with a comparison he had done nothing to merit.

Just a few weeks ago, there had been a terrible storm raging at the time Bess had gone to bed. Even behind the thick walls of Hanley Castle, Bess was afraid of the thunder and lightning, but she had said nothing, ashamed that a girl of her age, and a twice-married one at that, should have such a fear. Yet Hugh had guessed her secret. "Shall I stay awhile? I haven't in some time," he had said. Then he had climbed into bed and held her, stroking her hair and squeezing her hand each time a clap of thunder or a bolt of lightning made her flinch. By the time the storm abated, she had fallen fast asleep in his embrace.

Much later during the night, the storm nothing more than a gentle shower of rain now, she had awoken and realized that she was not alone in her bed. Hugh, fully dressed, lay beside her;

evidently he had drifted off while holding her. She had studied him shyly as he slept, turning aside and feigning sleep when he began to stir. Then she had heard him sit up and quietly make his way out of her chamber, but not before he had leaned over and kissed her on the cheek. What if he had known that she was awake? Perhaps one thing might have led to another and they would not be in such misery now.

She could still make it right, she realized with relief. She would go to his chamber and apologize, and if he still wanted her, she would give herself to him. If his ardor had passed, perhaps at least they could sleep side by side and wake in the morning as friends.

Bess slid out of bed, grabbed a lantern, and went to Hugh's chamber, where she pushed open an outer door. Between that and an inner door were sleeping two young pages on pallets. One of them sat up and blinked, then muttered, "My lady, you can't—"

"Of course I can. Hugh is my husband."

The half-awake page being too dazed to muster a coherent argument, Bess swept past him and opened the door to Hugh's chamber. It was strange, she reflected, that she had been in his sleeping quarters at his various castles only one or two times. How could she have been so incurious about the man? She pushed open the heavy bed curtains and looked down at her husband. Hugh had once told her that between his prison years and his years of soldiering he had learned the knack of sleeping anywhere at any time the opportunity presented itself, and once asleep, he slept soundly. Evidently he had not been exaggerating, and the wine had probably helped on this night, for he did not stir at her approach. Bess reached to nudge him awake— shyly, because his bare chest and arms indicated that he was one of those who preferred to sleep in his skin alone—and then froze as she saw what the faint light had not revealed before: a sandy-haired figure next to Hugh, rising up on one elbow.

"Mother of God," whispered Emma.

Bess slammed her hand against Emma's cheek just as Hugh stirred. "Er?" He blinked. "Oh."

Bess turned and fled the room.

Only at dawn, when the manor began to come to life, did she stop sobbing into her pillow. She rolled over onto her back and listened as people scurried about outside, inside, in her own chamber. Someone, probably Mary, called, "My lady?"

"My head aches. Go away. I wish to rest in peace and quiet."

Never had she spoken so snappishly to Mary before.

A clinking outside her bed curtains indicated that ale and bread were being brought to her to break her fast, but she ignored the sounds and the pleasant smells that were filling her room and continued to lie staring at her bed canopy. The sun was higher, and Bess still in bed, when she heard another step, one she knew well by now. Hugh parted the bed curtains. "Bess?"

"I have nothing to say to you."

"Well, I do to you. We're getting ready to leave."

"Who? You and your whore?"

"My men and I."

"Be gone, then."

"So I shall. Good-bye."

He let the bed curtain that he had pushed aside fall back into place, and in a moment Bess heard her chamber door closing firmly. Not even the commotion of Hugh and his men's departure some minutes later tempted Bess out of bed.

It was an hour or so later that a knock sounded at her chamber door. Lady Welles's voice called, "May I come in, my lady?"

"Yes."

She let Emma do the work of pulling back the bed curtains and fastening them against the posts. When Emma was done, she said, "I have come to tell you that I shall be leaving for my own home, my lady. With your permission I will send for my things later, when I can hire a cart. It is difficult today because so many have gone to the ports for this affair in Brittany."

Bess was faintly pleased to see the beginnings of a bruise where she had slapped Emma's cheek. "Has this been going on under my nose since I married Hugh?"

"No. All was at an end until last night. I will swear to it."

"He had a lover before he married, I have heard. That was you?"

"Yes. For many years."

"And that was why you wanted to come into our household. To be near him."

"You know that is not true. I came against my better judgment because you invited me and I liked you. And he consented to my coming against *his* better judgment because it was something you were set on and because he wanted to make you happy. It meant nothing to him, what happened last night. He never intended to hurt you."

"So he was so concerned with my feelings that he spent the night with you." Bess was having a hard time preserving her hauteur. Her lip wobbled.

"Only when you refused to lie with him as his wife. You hurt him to the very bone with that."

"He told you so?"

"No. I knew it. He'd been hoping for so much when he came to your chamber last night—I could tell from his face when he walked in. Good Lord, Bess! I doubt he had been with anyone since we parted before your marriage. When he walked out of your chamber he looked like a beaten dog. I followed him; I couldn't bear to see him look so miserable. I followed him to his chamber. All he would say was, 'She hates me, Emma. I've tried my best and there's nothing more I can do.' I put my hand on his shoulder to comfort him and nature took its course."

Bess said, "I didn't mean to be unkind! But he was tipsy and I was tired and my head hurt. And my monthly course was coming on to boot. If he'd only been patient."

"He has been patient. And since he fell in love with you it has been harder for him."

"In love with me?"

"Bess, I have known Hugh since we were children. I was his lover when you were still a little child. I told him when he and I parted that he was falling in love with you, and I was right. It is not in his nature to live with a pretty young woman day after day and not to love her. Have you never noticed the looks he gives you?"

Bess shook her head.

"Then you are foolish and inattentive. Every time he sits at table with you, he looks at you as if he were a lovesick boy. His eyes follow you across the room, wherever you go. He can't stop admiring you." She waved her hand at the luxurious furnishings of Bess's chamber. "Look at this! He's tried so hard to please you; he's given you everything you ask him for. And what have you given him in return?"

Tears were falling silently down Bess's face. She wiped them with her sleeve and said, "I did not mean to hurt him, Emma. Truly I did not. I—like him. But I was tired—and scared."

"Scared?"

"Joan said it hurt."

Emma shook her head pityingly. "Bess, Hugh took my maidenhead and it hurt not a whit. True, I was older than you and far less shy of him. But you have nothing to dread with Hugh. He would not be rough with you, ever. He cherishes you. Trust me."

Bess's spirit began to return. "I would have found that out last night, perhaps, if you had not been in his bed."

Emma winced. "True." She sighed. "I have been harsh with you, haven't I? We were all three at fault, me most of all. I could have refused him and did not."

Bess's tears started to fall afresh. "And now everything is ruined. Isn't it?"

"No. He came to your chamber this morning, didn't he?"

"Yes, and he was cold to me. I was hateful to him."

"Still, he could not bring himself to go without saying goodbye." Emma smiled at Bess. "He loves you, Bess. He will be back. And then the two of you can start afresh. What happened between him and me will never happen again." She stood and said after an awkward pause, "I shall begin packing my things now."

"Please don't. Please stay."

"Bess?"

"There is no reason why you should go because I pushed Hugh into your bed." She stared at the coverlet. "And I would miss you. We have become friends."

Emma smiled wryly. "Me into his bed, to be precise. And I have repaid your friendship ill, I fear." Her expression turned serious. "Bess, if that is how you feel, I should be honored to stay. I have been happy here, and I would miss you very much too." She patted Bess's hand. "But I will leave when Hugh returns. With you being a true wife to him then he will want no other woman, but it is better for all that I go, I think. Perhaps I will let him find a husband for me as he offered."

"Then it is settled. Now please help me dress so that I can break my fast. I am famished."

Bess slid out of bed and Emma began to help her into her clothes. Then Bess turned pale. "Emma?"

"Yes, dear?"

"What if he does not come back? What if something hap—"

Emma wrapped her arms around Bess. "We must pray hard that does not happen, the two of us and everyone else here. And if God is merciful, He will heed our prayers."

5

July 1342 to March 1343

In his prison days, one of Hugh's pastimes had been to choose a wife for himself. He'd not based his choice on his situation as the imprisoned son of an attainted traitor, of course, for that narrowed his range of options, to put it mildly. Instead, he'd assumed that his father and grandfather were alive and thriving (he had the right to set the parameters of his own pastime, after all) and that his father's criteria would dutifully have to be followed. The girl had to be from a noble family, preferably an earl's daughter or better; no humble knight's daughters need apply. An heiress would be preferable, but was not mandatory. As royal connections were more than welcome, English birth was not imperative; foreign royalty or nobility would make an interesting possibility. To these paternal criteria Hugh added his own special requirements: nearness to Hugh's own age, ample breasts, a sweet smile, and an eagerness to engage in all sorts of bed tricks in all positions and at all times. In Bristol Castle, by far the worst of his prisons until Mortimer's fall had eased his lot, he'd sit on the floor of his cell in the semi-darkness, ill-fed, ill-clothed, and chilly, his pale, thin face intent with concentration as he tried to pick a suitable bride. It was not a task he took lightly; this was a lady he would have to spend his life with. He could spend hours debating with himself on the subject, sometimes becoming so engrossed in his imaginary dilemma that he would fail to respond to a question or to a command and would have to be nudged back to reality by his guards. Such reminders might take the form of a gentle tap on the shoulder or a kick, depending on the guard. If it were the latter, it would lead to a second means by which Hugh had passed the time at Bristol: fighting with his guards. And as he was invariably outnumbered, a third occupation flowed naturally from the second: nursing his wounds.

Well, at least the fighting had helped him on the battlefield. But the marriage game hadn't prepared him at all for Bess. If only he had chosen her as carefully as he had his imaginary bride.

Did the girl know how pretty she had become? At the time of their first meeting, Hugh had thought her a pleasant-looking lass, who would without doubt grow into a reasonably attractive woman, but something had happened to her recently, something Hugh had not predicted. In a matter of a few months, she'd shot up tall and filled out, and her facial proportions had changed somehow so that her huge, expressive brown eyes dominated her serious face, turning it into one that Hugh found to be haunting and irresistible. Her long, thick hair, a rich brown in color, which had been her chief attraction when Hugh had first seen her, had not altered, but now that she had adopted the married woman's custom of hiding it in public, it had become a mysterious thing to be seen only at night when Hugh visited her. Too often for his comfort lately, he'd imagined it spread out over her pillow as she lay on her bed without a stitch on, awaiting his pleasure.

God almighty.

Now that Hugh recalled it, his father had almost married him to an Elizabeth Comyn, a woman eight years his senior and one of the heirs of the late Earl of Pembroke. Hugh doubted that the lady had been enthralled with the idea of marrying a cub like himself—he'd been only seventeen at the time—though her opinion would have counted for naught, of course. Hugh himself had not heard of the plan until it had been abandoned; whether his own objections would have counted either, he did not know. Something had put his father off the idea, most likely the fact that the unfortunate Elizabeth had given up her lands to him without him having to go to the trouble of getting her for a daughter-in-law. (Probably his father would have found a disinherited heiress rather poor company as his son's bride; in his own way he had liked harmonious family relations.) Having survived this plucking by Hugh's father, Elizabeth had married a Richard Talbot and had been restored to her lands at the time of the queen's invasion. Hugh had often wondered if his father had had other brides for him in mind, but aside from their stilted last conversation at Caerphilly Castle, the subject had not been seriously raised.

In any event, Hugh's father could not have picked for Hugh worse than Hugh had picked for himself. A pretty, spoiled wench whose beautiful body aroused him unbearably and who loathed the sight of him.

Elizabeth Comyn would have been better.

"Hugh! I've called your name twice. What's on your mind, that you've lost your hearing?"

The man riding up beside him was none other than Richard Talbot. Hugh could hardly tell him that he had been wondering what would have happened if he had married Richard's wife. "Sorry."

"You're missing that young wife of yours," said Talbot. "Indisposed, was she?"

"Yes."

"Who knows, Despenser? You might have an heir waiting for you when you return."

"No, she said it was a bad cold," said Hugh hastily. No point in telling Richard that his wife would not let him near her without raising a ruckus, but also no point in starting an impossible rumor. Richard was a gossip.

Richard would not be stopped. "That's how I started out, I hear, as a cold."

Hugh and Richard had started their rather unlikely friendship when Richard had served as one of Hugh's mainprisors after he'd been provisionally released from prison and was awaiting a final pardon from the king. The mutual liking that had grown between them had been strong enough to overcome the grudge that Richard might have justly held against the Despenser family for the harsh treatment of Elizabeth Comyn. The lady herself was still a little frosty with Hugh, though he'd gotten a chuckle out of her the last time he'd visited at Goodrich Castle.

"Who's ill?" Oliver Ingham, seneschal of Aquitaine, rode up with a frown. He was an even more incongruous companion for Hugh than Talbot, for Ingham, though he'd gotten on well with the Despensers and the second Edward in their day, had jumped ship at the precisely right moment and had ended up as a member of Roger Mortimer's inner circle. So close had he been, in fact, that he'd been arrested at the same time Mortimer had. Yet within a few weeks he'd been freed, and by the next summer he had been reappointed to his old post in Aquitaine and had been there ever since, save for the occasional trip to England like the one he was taking now to bring back troops.

"Despenser's wife," said Richard with a wink.

Ingham missed the wink. He was a crotchety man, a trait that Hugh would have attributed to age and failing health had not he known that Ingham had been no less cranky in his prime twenty years before. Perhaps, thought Hugh, he had assimilated to new regimes so readily because he treated everyone pretty much in the same manner: as a child who needed a good talking to. "Don't tell me you are planning on heading back to her, Despenser. We need to be setting off."

"She's fine. It's just a summer cold," said Hugh wearily.

Ingham nodded and began telling Hugh what he had already told him—he was a man who tended to repeat himself—but Hugh did not protest, as Ingham's droning allowed him to think his own thoughts. Since the Count of Montfort had been imprisoned, the Countess of Montfort had taken over the command of his force. "It's said that when Blois's troops arrived in Hennebont, she rode through the streets, urging her men to victory. And a victory they had—for the time being anyway. Killed the French whoresons by the score. But they came back and tried to besiege the place. Damned if they didn't give it up, though. Cowards."

"And the countess? Where is she now?"

"Brest, with none but Walter Mauny's men to help her. Our king promised thousands, and where the hell are they?" He shook his head with disgust. "She can't hold out forever."

Why not? Hugh thought. Bess certainly could.

"THE WORST PART about being besieged," said Edward le Despenser a month or so later, "is not being able to send a letter to Anne. Or to receive one."

Hugh without thinking very hard about the issue could have come up with even worse things about being besieged, such as starving to death or being taken captive, but he forbore to point them out to his brother at the present time. Instead, he confined himself to a sympathetic nod.

Ingham and Hugh had been bound for Gascony, but upon landing at Saint-Mathieu and seeing how vulnerable the countess's position in Brest was, it had been decided that Hugh and his eighty or so men would stay to aid her. He had arrived just in time, for by August Brest was surrounded, shadowed by fourteen Genoese galleys in its harbor and ringed by French troops on the land. More English troops were on the way, Hugh had kept assuring the countess, but there was no sign of their approaching. In the meantime, those in Brest had little to do but wait for their relief. Hugh had been through this long before at Caerphilly Castle, but Edward had not, and the strain was beginning to tell on both him and Gilbert, who was also serving in Hugh's retinue. Pleased as Hugh was to have them with him, he was relieved in a way that John, his youngest full brother, was in the queen's household and that William, his half-brother, was safely at Glastonbury Abbey, where he was to become one of the monks. Two brothers to worry about were enough.

Hugh pointed out the window toward the row of Genoese galleys. Bobbing in the water, they made a pretty picture; sunk beneath the waves, they would have made an even prettier one.

"Pity our father isn't here. He pirated one of them, do you remember? He'd have kept them from ever reaching the port."

"One pirate in the family is enough," said Edward. He had begun to pace around the room. "What if she's with child?"

"Then you'll have a pleasant surprise waiting for you when you return to England."

"Aren't you worried about Bess? What if she's with child?"

The two older brothers being alone together, Hugh said, "There's only been one virgin birth known to man, Edward."

This confidence at least made Edward stop pacing. "What? You haven't—"

"She's put herself off limits." Hugh decided it was his turn to pace.

"Surely she's old enough?" Edward saw the look on Hugh's face. "I'm sorry, Hugh. I don't mean to pry."

"It's one way to pass the time." He shrugged. "I came to her bed the night before we left Ashley. She sent me packing. Obviously, the girl is oblivious to my charms."

"Had you been getting along?"

"So I thought. The girl's never been madly in love with me; I knew that from the start. But I thought she was thawing. And then—"

"You must have taken her by surprise," said Edward. "Women have strange moods, Hugh. Even Anne does. We've quarreled during them."

"You and Anne have quarreled?"

Edward's face took on a look of deep concentration. "Two or three times," he admitted after thinking for a while.

Hugh snorted. "I wonder Anne hasn't sought an annulment." He shook his head. "I keep telling myself that, Edward, that it was just a mood of Bess's. I was a little tipsy, too; that puts her off, I know. Maybe I shouldn't have surprised her; maybe I should have told her before what my intentions were so that she could commiserate with her ladies first." He grimaced. "Of course, I didn't help matters by lying with Emma later that night. My only lapse since we married, but Bess caught me."

"Christ, man! How drunk were you?"

"Not much at all, not enough to make an excuse of it. Just acting like a tom fool." He drummed his finger on a ledge. "Now I wonder if I'll even have a wife to come home to."

"You will, Hugh. She can't hold one night against you, surely."

"You might be underestimating my Bess." Hugh half smiled. "But aside from that, I keep thinking, what if the girl just can't abide me? What if it's a marriage like poor Isabel's to Arundel, or like Mother's cousin Joan of Bar to the Earl of Surrey, or like our grandfather Gilbert de Clare's marriage to that Alice de Lusignan?" He eyed the ships again and lowered his voice. "Except that in those marriages the loathing was mutual, and I've come to love Bess, Edward. Much as I loved Emma, I love Bess more." Hugh shook his head. "Jesus, I'm rattling on, aren't I?"

"It will come aright, Hugh. I'm certain of it. Bess is a sweet girl. She's young, that's all, barely out of childhood, really. I was lucky that Anne was ripe for marriage when I met her." He smiled. "She's so beautiful. I still can't believe that she chose to have me for a husband."

"I can't believe it either," Hugh said, relieved to be falling back into this joshing mode, for taking advice from his younger brother had been rather unnerving. Still, Edward had cheered him considerably. "Shall we wager whether your Anne will deliver yet another boy to the world?"

From high atop the castle there came shouts, followed by a peal of bells. The door banged open, and Gilbert ran inside. "They've spotted ships! English ones."

IN THE MONTHS TO COME, when the nightmares that had plagued Hugh in his younger days had come back in full force, Hugh would wake, catch his breath, and then take his mind back slowly over the weeks that passed from August 18, 1342, when the Earl of Northampton's fleet arrived at Brest, to September 30, 1342. Somewhere in his mind, he supposed, was the hope that perhaps he was remembering something wrong and that the day had not happened as he remembered it at all.

Once in Brest that August day, the Earl of Northampton's fleet had made short work of the port's besiegers. The crews of the Genoese ships, trapped between the English ships and Brest Castle's garrison, fled, leaving the earl and his men to set them afire. The French troops on the land, seeing the approach of well over two hundred ships and assuming that they carried an army far larger than their own, retreated.

Hugh and his men joined Northampton's army, which proceeded toward the town of Morlaix. When they arrived there on September 3, they tried to take the town, but its defenders would not budge. So Hugh's men, so recently besieged themselves, became the besiegers now, alongside the earl's troops.

The Count of Blois, however, had his own plans for Morlaix. Hoping to trap Northampton's men with his army on one side and the walls of Morlaix on the other, he had moved his troops close to Lanmeur when Northampton, getting word of Blois's intentions, lifted the siege and moved in Blois's direction. Having found a spot to Northampton's liking, between a road and a thick woods, the English troops awaited battle there, using their time well by digging a trench and then concealing it with greenery. The covered trench was a trick that had been played on the English at the terrible battle of Bannockburn, and although few of the men at Morlaix were old enough to have fought there, they had grown up listening to the rueful recollections of their fathers and grandfathers and had determined not to repeat their mistakes.

Then they waited for the French to arrive, which they did the next morning, September 30. Northampton's men, knights and common soldiers alike, were on foot. Watching the three columns of French troops approaching, Hugh realized that the three thousand English troops were outnumbered, though how badly was anyone's guess. Four to one? Three to one? A mere two to one? Hugh could not tell, and as much confidence as he had in the abilities of his able cousin Northampton, and even in his own, he was nonetheless grateful that there had been time for confession that morning. Yet as the first column of men approached on foot, they were forced back by a stream of English arrows. So soon had the French been stopped in their tracks that it appeared that none of them had even discovered the concealed trench. There followed a seemingly endless pause for consultation between Blois and his leaders that the unscathed English filled with nervous jokes. "What the hell are they *doing*?" Edward asked.

"Drawing a map showing every brothel within the vicinity," Hugh speculated.

"That's the type of assault they're best suited for," said Talbot.

He had barely finished speaking when a mass of horsemen stampeded toward the English. For a moment, it seemed that all the digging, all the careful disguising with vegetation and twigs had been in vain; then at last, there were cries, curses, whinnies as one horse after another fell into the trench and as more men were shoved forward by the press of the forces behind them.

And then a group of French soldiers, perhaps two hundred in all, somehow evaded the trench and charged, straight toward Hugh's men. Hugh's archers were ready for them, holding their barrage of arrows until the French were well within killing range. Then they let them fly. The field by Hugh was a chaos of dying horses and dying men, yet some of the French pushed through and slashed at Hugh's knights, who paid them back in kind. Hugh groaned as one of his knights, fighting hand to hand with a man he'd unhorsed, fell, but he soon had the satisfaction of dispatching his own opponent, then another, before Northampton's reserves streamed in, surrounding the French soldiers.

Then the sounds of fighting ceased. There were only the moans of the injured, the pants of the English gasping for breath, the orders barked out to the French prisoners. Hugh raised his helm and looked around. Most of the bodies fallen around him were French. Only the one English knight lay dead. Two squires bent over him, obscuring the surcoat that he wore over his armor. Then one turned. "Sir Hugh! It's your—"

Edward.

Hugh leaned on his sword, feeling the same sick sensation he had experienced when he heard Felton's news at Caerphilly Castle sixteen years before. Beside him, he heard Richard Talbot mutter, "Shit."

A trumpet sounded. Hugh realized for the first time that he had been wounded in the leg, but he noted the pain with the same detachment as he did everything else as he limped over to Northampton. "We've killed our fair share, but there's still a bloody lot of them left, and still more than us," the earl said. "We've few arrows and little time to retrieve the ones we've shot. We'd be suicidal to stay out there. Agreed?"

Every captain, Hugh included, nodded.

"Then we'll retreat, back into those woods. Men facing in every direction. If they follow, they'll have us facing toward them from all sides with our swords."

"Like a hedgehog," said Hugh.

Northampton snorted. "Good one, Hugh." He cleared his throat. "You lost a knight?"

"His brother Sir Edward," Talbot answered for him.

"Whoresons," said Northampton. His own brother Edward, his twin, had drowned during a Scottish campaign eight years before. "I'm sorry, Hugh."

Hugh nodded. He did not trust himself to speak again.

Yet when he walked away from Northampton he heard himself giving orders anew, just as if this were any other battle. He and the rest of Northampton's men retreated into the forest as planned, leaving the field strewn with corpses, Edward's among them.

Blois's men tried to penetrate the forest, but as Northampton had predicted, had no luck and finally retreated, turning back the way they had come. The English had won in a sense, it seemed, though they by now were too famished and exhausted to enjoy the outcome by whatever name it was called. They drew back to the town of Morlaix.

They had encamped and rounded up some semblance of food when the supply wagons they had left behind them rumbled into the camp, bearing wounded men and, in the last wagon, Edward's body. Hugh, standing by Edward's squire and Gilbert, gazed down at the brother to whom he'd been closest, trying not to look at the wound to the head, inflicted by a mace, that mercifully must have killed Edward almost instantly. As Hugh bowed his head, trying to summon a prayer but unable to think of any words but curses, the squire gently tugged at a fine cord around Edward's neck. "His lady will be wanting this, my lord."

He handed Hugh a silk pouch, sewn to the cord. Nothing appeared to be in the pouch, so light was it, but Hugh opened it anyway and pulled out a thick strand of curly, golden hair, undoubtedly Anne's. It was knotted by a thread to three finer strands of hair, presumably the boys'. "He wore it whenever he fought."

"For good luck, I suppose?"

"Why, yes, my lord."

Edward's squire evidently possessed as little sense of the ironic as Edward had himself. Hugh smiled. "Thank you." Then he went to his tent, where he put his head in his hands and wept until he could weep no more.

THE KING HIMSELF arrived in Brittany several weeks later. Northampton and his men had moved to Brest, where the king and his men joined them.

Among the men who had sailed with the king was William de Montacute. With Edward's death, Hugh's marital woes had been pushed far from his mind, and he did not even remember until he and William were standing side by side that William, who was less than a decade older than Hugh, was his father-in-law. Having recalled this fact to his memory, Hugh then asked about Bess, but in a tone so perfunctory that William might have taken offense had he not known that Hugh had lost a brother three weeks before. "She's doing well," William assured him.

"Is she with your lady wife, do you know?"

"No. She said she would stay on your estates."

This surprised Hugh, who had assumed that Bess would take the first opportunity to get off the Despenser estates that she could. "I hope it doesn't get lonely for her," he said politely.

"Well, she said that her ladies were good company."

Hugh flinched, thinking of his last night with Emma. Had Bess told her father of his behavior? Evidently not, or her father would not be speaking so cordially to him.

He was glad when the king called the men to him and began laying plans.

The king decided to turn his attention to besieging Vannes, but had little success. In the meantime, he sent Northampton, the Earl of Warwick, and Hugh to attack Nantes and the surrounding countryside. The king's orders had been to spare nothing, and Hugh had no desire to contravene them. He would not countenance rape, but he let his men loot what they wanted to and burn whatever was of no use to them. It was some recompense for the corpse that was now buried in a little churchyard near Morlaix, far from all those his brother had loved.

Hugh and his men spent Christmas and the New Year shivering outside Nantes, wondering what was going to happen next. The English were short of men, as they had always been, while word had it that more French troops were on the way. But the French had lost heart, it seemed. When papal officials arrived on the scene, both sides were willing to negotiate. By January 19, a truce had been concluded, and a month later, the English, along with the Countess of Montfort and her small children, were boarding the ships to take them to England.

It was on that voyage back that Hugh came as close as he ever had to dying. He was as far from caring as he ever had been. The brisk winds that aided them out of the harbor turned to deadly gales as they entered the open sea, and Hugh watched helplessly as one English ship, then another was engulfed by the waves and sank. Two of the crew on his own vessel were swept overboard. Where the ship carrying the king had been blown to no one knew; was it possible that they would come home—if they did come home—to an England ruled by a child? But finally the wind and waves died down, and the coast of England came into view. He was home, for what that was worth.

Reaching the shore, he found that the Countess of Montfort's ship was close behind his own, so naturally he stayed to offer what assistance he could. Soon he saw the figures of a woman and two small children being helped into a boat and rowed to shore. As the boat pulled closer, he could see their features clearly. The two children had looks of terror on their faces, a natural reaction for anyone who had just crossed in such conditions to have. The countess, by contrast, bore not a trace of expression, not even when it was at last time for her to disembark. She stepped out of the boat without looking around her, and she ignored Hugh and all of the officials who had gathered to pay their respects. This was not like her at all, Hugh knew. Joan of Flanders was the most affable and gracious of women. Had not she rallied her troops at Hennebont with her courage and charm?

Behind the countess was one of her knights, a man Hugh had come to know at Brest. He met Hugh's eyes. "Mad," he whispered. "Gone stark mad on the crossing."

Hugh looked again at the countess and saw that the man was right; her eyes were looking at nothing. It was all he could do to keep from slapping the woman—either in anger or in an attempt to beat some sanity into her, he did not know. He knew only that Edward, and many others, and most recently the men lying at the bottom of the Channel, had died for a madwoman's cause. For nothing.

THE KING, it turned out, was alive and suitably grateful for it; he would be giving thanks first in London, then at the second Edward's tomb at Gloucester. Hugh could have joined him; his father-in-law was with him, and Gloucester of course was close to Hugh's own estates. But he was not in the mood for thanksgiving. In January, he had sent a message asking Bess to await him at Cardiff, a place he had chosen for no better reason than that it was about as far away from Brittany as he could get, he supposed. To Wales, therefore, he went straightaway in March instead of tarrying with the king's party.

The townspeople greeted him warmly when he passed through the gates of Cardiff, a welcome that would have been deeply moving to him at another time, for his father had left him a legacy of mistrust by his Welsh tenants that had taken Hugh years to overcome. He managed what he hoped was a convincing smile and rode through the gatehouse to Cardiff Castle. His arrival had been heralded, for the bailey was crowded with people standing at attention.

Anne, Edward's widow, was among them. Hugh was relieved to see that she was dressed in mourning. Although he had sent a man to break the news to her, he'd not known whether the fellow had made it safely across the Channel. He had dreaded that she might be expecting Edward to be among the men returning. Anne's two elder sons stood beside her, and the third was holding the hand of his nurse. And, just as his brother had predicted, there was a fourth child in her belly, Hugh saw as he drew closer. At least Edward had spent his last nights in England enjoyably.

He dismounted and embraced his sister-in-law. "I'm so sorry, Anne." His voice broke, and he paused to command it again. "His squire has some of his belongings for you. His sword and a keepsake. I wish I could have brought his body back, but it was impossible under the circumstances. We did see to it that he had a proper burial."

"I know, Hugh. And he left something more of him behind." Anne managed a smile and patted her belly.

Hugh stooped and put an arm around each of his older nephews. They looked grieved, but also rather self-important, so much so that Hugh nearly smiled. "Your father was a fine, brave knight. He died in the thick of battle, like your great-great-

grandfather Hugh, fighting to the very last. I saw him fall myself. You can be proud of him, as he was proud of you. Will you
always remember that?"

They nodded, looking even more self-satisfied than ever, and
Hugh rose. Then Alice, having pushed to the forefront of the
crowd under the pretext of helping Anne le Despenser's nurse-
maid with the three small boys, gave Hugh a little shove. More
than anyone else in Hugh's household, Alice knew the dismal
state of his marriage, being the one who washed the couple's
sheets and saw, day after day, no sign that their match had been
consummated. "Sir," she whispered. "Please see to your lady
wife. She needs you too."

For the first time, Hugh thought of Bess. He had to look then
to find her. Though she was a tall girl, who had grown a little
since Hugh had last seen her, she had almost disappeared into
the throng, having stood back instead taking her place at the fore
as the lady of the household. "My lady," he said politely.

"My lord." She stepped forward and Hugh realized that in
his anger at her rejection of him, he had forgotten how young
and fresh she was; in his mind, he had built her into some sort of
hardened Jezebel. He bent his head to kiss her politely, purely
for appearances' sake, but she flung her arms around him, almost knocking him backward. "I missed you so," she whispered

Hugh stood stunned for a moment, then returned her embrace. He stepped back and looked into Bess's eyes. They were
brimming with tears, he saw before she turned her gaze to the
ground. He despised himself, suddenly, for the letters he'd sent
to her occasionally; letters of business without a hint of warmth
in them. What could he have been thinking? Hugh lifted her chin
with his finger and smiled at her, then reached for her again,
oblivious of the bystanders, who in any case were quietly dis-
persing, leaving an ever widening space between them and their
lord and lady whom all knew had parted so angrily and needed
so badly to reconnect somehow.

As he held her trembling figure he forgot for the first time
the visions that had haunted him since he had returned to Eng-

land: Edward's dead body lying in the field of Morlaix, the Countess of Montfort's expressionless face. Here was something worth fighting for, he realized, something pure and innocent remaining amid all the madness and death in the world, something to protect and cherish always. It was worth risking all to see that she and those like her lived their days peacefully and securely.

"I've missed you too, sweetheart," he said, realizing as he did that he was telling the perfect truth. As he held her and kissed her, feeling her hot tears falling onto his neck, he sensed that his own were coming on as well. Then he suddenly became conscious, for the first time in months, of his muddy, sweat-stained clothing, his unkempt beard, and the horsy smell that must be emanating from him and all the others. He drew a shaky breath and smiled. "Will you order me a bath, Bess?"

As Hugh's barber transformed him from a hairy savage into the Lord of Glamorgan, Bess settled into a window seat and sat there quietly. A series of servants filled a tub with steaming water as Hugh's shorn hair fell to the floor. Bess averted her eyes as Hugh, the last of his clothes removed, stepped into his bath. He and his page had been scrubbing for some time when he said, "Bess, would you do my back?"

"Yes, Hugh."

Bess took the sponge the page gave her as if being handed a scorpion, but gamely began sponging his back as the page scampered off. "Bess, there is something we must talk about."

"Oh?" Bess's voice was calm, but she scrubbed a good deal harder.

"Lady Welles." This time the sponge rubbed so hard that Hugh winced. "Don't go lower down, whatever you do," he said, and stood up. Bess again looked away as he wrapped a towel around himself and sat on a bench near the fire, then gestured for Bess to sit beside him. "I suppose by now you know what Lady Welles and I were to each other before you and I married?" She nodded. "We ended it when I married you, and we planned on keeping it that way. But that night I was mad with lust for you

116

and tipsy and full of hurt pride, and she was there wanting to comfort me. Neither of us intended it to end as it did." He sighed. "I should have gone to you straightaway after you found us, I suppose. But I was half ashamed, half pleased I'd hurt you as you'd hurt me. I was a fool, Bess."

Bess stared at the fire. "I understand why you did it, Hugh. I was dreadful. I should not have said that about your father, I know. But I was nervous, and you were half drunk, which made me more so. But I tried to make it right—"

"And then I wrecked it by being in bed with Emma when you came to me. Jesus, Bess! If I could live that night over again—"

"Me too. I was so worried I would never see you again, that I would never have a chance to make amends. I even thought you might be going to have the marriage annulled. Every day I've been half expecting to hear from the Pope."

"Annulled?"

"So you could marry Emma."

"Sweetheart." He chose his words carefully. "Bess, it's true, I would have made her my wife if things were different. I did love her. I care deeply about her still; I'll look out for her always and make sure she wants for nothing. But it's you I've loved these last months. Even when I tried to pretend to myself I didn't."

"Truly, Hugh?"

"Truly, Bess."

He smiled at her, and she smiled back nervously. He would not take her by surprise as he had before, he decided. "Will you let me visit you tonight? I promise, I'll do nothing if you're uneasy. Perhaps we can start just by sharing a bed for a few nights. Even longer if you wish."

"I was thinking we could get it all over with now."

He laughed. "It's not like having a tooth drawn, sweetheart."

She blushed. "I didn't mean to sound—"

"I know. Well, then, stand up, Bess. Let me help you with your fastenings."

She stood with her back to him. Letting the towel he had knotted around his waist slip off, Hugh undressed her down to her shift. He had thought she might want to leave it on in bed, like some form of feminine armor, but she surprised him by wriggling out of it and then turning to face him, her eyes fixed firmly on his chest and venturing no lower. Unclothed, Bess was an exquisite sight, even more so than he had imagined, but Hugh said nothing. Then she abruptly turned and climbed into his bed. He followed and took her into his arms, feeling her stiffen in all of the wrong places as he did so.

It was not the most satisfactory of couplings. Fair as Bess was, the events of the last months had told on Hugh in more ways than one, and he found himself having to concentrate all of his mental efforts upon becoming aroused. Once he managed that, there was the new problem that with Emma, he'd had the great advantage of not knowing that he was taking a virgin; with Bess, he could do nothing without worrying that he was frightening or hurting her. Holding onto Hugh as determinedly as she might a troublesome horse, Bess took the loss of her maidenhead stoically enough, with a dignified little yelp of pain, after which Hugh was far too quick to achieve satisfaction, regrettably at the very instant that he sensed Bess beginning to relax a little underneath him and even to make a small noise that suggested interest, if not satisfaction. "I'm sorry, sweetheart. You're so beautiful that I was too quick. Next time will be more pleasurable for you. I promise."

"I thought it lasted quite long enough," she said politely.

He chuckled and rolled off her, then guided her so that she lay in the crook of his arm. "Well, at least we've given Alice her self-respect back. She'll be able to tell all and sundry that we've consummated the marriage at last." Their lovemaking, awkward as it had been, had made them much more at ease with each other, and they both were well content as they lay curled up together, listening to the rain that had begun to fall heavily outside. They had been lying that way for some time when Hugh raised up. "Bess. I almost fell asleep just now."

"So did I. It's pleasant lying here."

"I'm afraid if I do I might frighten you." He stared up at the bed canopy. "Since—since my brother died I have these nightmares. My pages tell me I scream like the devil himself was beside me some nights, that I wake them. I feel bad enough about inflicting myself on them. I don't want to do so with you."

"It will not frighten me. If I wake I will fall back asleep, that's all." She touched his cheek. "Tell me about your brother, Hugh. Perhaps that will help."

"What's to tell? I saw him fall. There wasn't a thing I could do to help him. I'd trained him well and he was fighting as ably as any of us. I didn't even know it was him until later." Hugh sighed. After a long pause, he said, "Bess, I feel so guilty."

"Because you couldn't keep him from harm?"

"No. He would have been humiliated if I'd tried to keep him from harm, thought of himself as less than a knight. There was nothing I could do. No, Bess."

"Then why, Hugh?"

"Back in Brittany, I thought that it should have been me; I'm more expendable. No children, just a wife who didn't care for me." He stopped Bess's indignant squawk of protest with a kiss, which she returned shyly. "I see now that I was wrong. But I still feel guilty because I've been given another chance and he wasn't. His family meant everything to him, and him to them."

They were silent for a long time. "Hugh, you must suppose the Lord meant something in taking him. It is not your fault that you were spared."

"Yes, I will have to try to think that." He reached for Bess again. "And with you lying here it's not so hard to do so now."

She kissed him, this time less shyly. Hugh in turn began moving his hands over her body, with none of the hesitation he had shown before. "Hugh!" she whispered as his hand went to her inner thigh and began to roam about.

He felt her begin to respond to him at last, just as he realized how intense his own longing had become. "The last time was for Alice, sweetheart. This time is for ourselves."

January 1344

Bess whispered to her sister-in-law, "I do not think you should call the dowager queen Isabella an old trout, Joan."

"But she's old, and she looks like a trout when she pinches her lips together like she's doing now. Therefore, she is an old trout."

"I think that's what they call a syllogism, Joan," said Bess, impressed for the moment. Then she added, "But I also think you have had too much wine. In fact, I am sure of it. You mustn't have any more."

"Oh, go to the devil, Bess."

"I'll drink yours so you can't have any more." Bess seized Joan's wine cup and drained it in a gulp, then leaned back, glowing with virtue as well as with wine even as Joan waved at a page to bring her some more.

The king had summoned all the great and most of the lesser lords of the land, along with their ladies, to Windsor Castle for a week of celebration and feasting. Bess had arrived with Hugh only that afternoon and had barely had time to unpack before the king had sent them a message: all of the ladies were to be entertained at a great feast just for them, with the men to be entertained in less grand style elsewhere. Each lady had been led into the hall by the king himself. Bess had been thrilled when the king commented on how lovely she was looking and on her new gown, which Bess's dressmaker had barely had time to finish in time for her to bring to court with her. The fact that the king had been heard to make such gallant comments to every woman he had escorted had not detracted from her pleasure in the least.

For many of the ladies, that had been quite a few cups of wine ago. Bess herself had had one or two more than usual, she would be the first to admit, but she was in far better condition than her sister-in-law and could therefore drink another with impunity, she decided. She beamed at the page who was filling her own cup, then winked at him. "I wish Hugh were here," she said after the page moved to another boisterous row of ladies.

"You always wish Hugh were here," said Joan. "Is he that good of a husband? I mean, where it matters?"

"What a question!" Bess glared at her wine cup. "Yes," she said, and giggled.

The last months had been happy ones for Bess. There had been no wars to take Hugh away from her, and when he went to Parliament soon after his return from Brittany, he'd taken Bess with him. In London they had stayed at his splendid home on the waterfront, where Bess could watch the ships coming and going from her window seat by day and spend her nights in Hugh's arms. She could not believe there had been a time when she had been cold to him as a husband. What a fool she had been!

Only one thing marred her happiness: she had not quickened with child. After those first few weeks of their reunion, when she and Hugh had made up for lost time by making love nearly every night, she had been certain that she would conceive and had been stunned to find her monthly course arriving at its accustomed time. She had not missed a month since then, except for one when she had been slightly late, and then as if to taunt her, her course had lasted longer than usual. Hugh had found her crying in their chamber that month. "Sweetheart. You are still very young. You will conceive yet."

"But what if I never do? What if I am barren?"

"Then we must learn to live with that."

121

"You won't cast me aside?"

"Bess! What rot. I love you. You know that."

"But you married because you wanted heirs . . ."

"Bess, I do. I won't deny I'll be disappointed if we have no children. But the land will stay in the Despenser family in any case. With Edward's four boys and my brothers, there's no chance that an outsider will inherit it. And if there were, well— you would still be my lady wife and my true love. Now come. Dry your eyes and let's go riding. When you're at last great with child, I won't let you on a horse, you know."

She had obeyed. But each month she still felt the same hope, and then the same disappointment. The latter had been especially keen just a few days before when Emma, who soon after Hugh's return from overseas had married one of Hugh's knights, had been delivered of a fine boy. Bess and Hugh, the godparents, had given the couple some fine plate as christening gifts, and Bess had embroidered a beautiful swaddling blanket for the child, but with each stitch, her heart had ached. When would she sew things for her own baby?

Joan had not conceived either, as far as Bess knew, but she did not seem overly bothered about it. "There's time," she had said offhandedly when Bess had brought up the subject delicately much earlier in the evening.

Bess sighed and took another long drink of wine, then followed Joan's eyes up to the dais where they kept roaming. As Joan had noted, up there were not only Queen Philippa and her oldest daughter, the Lady Isabella, but Isabella's rarely seen namesake, the dowager queen. None of the younger ladies in the great hall could keep from looking at her for long. Not only had she been an adulteress, which was wicked enough, but there were rumors that she had been a murderess as well, conniving with her lover to kill the poor imprisoned second Edward. The present king claimed that Mortimer alone had been responsible, but Bess had her doubts, and Joan had none whatsoever. "After all, she ordered that my own father be executed," she whispered, discreetly for a change.

"But she looks so beautiful," Bess whispered back. In fact, she could no longer make out the queen's features that distinctly, but earlier in the evening, she had noted that Isabella's face, though not a young one—she was in her late forties now—was still a very handsome one, notwithstanding the occasional trout-like expression she did assume when gazing in the direction of the giggling younger ladies. "I just can't believe she could kill her own husband."

"And speaking of Hugh, you know what she did to Hugh's father!"

"Hush, Joan. Here comes the king." Bess took a big gulp of wine to give her courage to face the king, of whom she was a bit shy.

Having dined with the men after seating the ladies, Edward had returned and was now strolling up and down the lines of tables, chatting and occasionally bestowing kisses on his prettiest female subjects. Bess had seen him talking with her mother up at the row of countesses near the dais, a row that was decidedly more somber and sober than the row on which Bess was sitting, designated for earls' daughters and the wives of the richer lords. Perhaps the nearby queens had had a dampening effect on the countesses, Bess thought. She was grateful that the countesses were seated at such an angle that her mother and Joan's could not see them.

The king ambled over. Though an amazing variety of food and wine had been carried to the ladies, it appeared that the men had had plenty at their feast as well, for when Edward bent and put one arm around Bess and the other around Joan, his breath smelled as strongly of wine as did Joan's. "Fair ladies," he said. "Are *you* enjoying yourselves?"

"Very much, your grace," said Bess, though the "your grace" sounded strangely even in her ears like "your glace." She giggled and tried it again. "Your glaze. I am delighted to be here, and have been enjoying the entertainment extremely well."

The king laughed and patted her hand. "Why, Bess, I suspect you've been enjoying my wine as well as my minstrels. I wager your Hugh will have his hands full tonight." He turned and kissed Joan, who, however, turned her face so that she kissed the king on the lips. "My," said Edward. "Young Montacute is a lucky man."

"I always wanted to do that," said Joan as the king moved away.

Jealous, Bess drank a consolatory cup of wine and made a conscientious effort to focus her attention on the court fool, though it was difficult to do with the room spinning and the fool multiplying himself before her eyes. She could not have said afterward how she managed to get up when the tables were moved for dancing, or how she found herself in the midst of a group of people dancing, the lords having come in to join the ladies. Even more baffling was how she ended up dancing with the king himself, leading him in a country dance picked up from some of Hugh's tenants. Difficult as she found it to walk in her state, she was somehow able to dance easily, so much so that a clapping little crowd gathered to watch, surrounding her and Edward and shielding them from the view of the throng in the hall. Only when the music stopped did she stumble into the king, who laughed and took her in his arms. "Do I get *my* kiss now?" she asked as she caught her breath.

"Your kiss?"

"You kissed Joan and not me. And I am as loyal a subject as she. It is unwise to play favorites, your glaze."

"True. How remiss of me," said Edward. He bent and kissed her on the lips, hard. "You're delectable," he whispered, not particularly softly. "Absolutely delectable." He smiled at her and stood back. "Is my subject pleased now?"

"Very much so." She curtseyed deeply and fell into the king again when she struggled to her feet. "I'm eager to serve you in every way," she said.

"I'll remember that," promised Edward. He kissed Bess again, then carefully set her on her feet a little ways off and turned to another partner. Bess accepted a cup from a grinning page and took a large drink from it. Then she gasped as someone put an arm around her and began hustling her away, having wrenched the cup out of her hands first. "Gilbert!" she said indignantly, recognizing her abductor as one of her brothers-in-law. "The feast has not ended yet!"

Gilbert le Despenser was one of the king's household knights. He was only in his early twenties, considerably younger than Hugh, and was said to resemble his mother much more strongly than his father. He was burlier than Hugh, with a few freckles and hair that was more red than auburn; a suitable look, Bess thought groggily, for someone who had been born during his father's pirate days. "For you it has," he said. "How much wine *have* you had?"

Bess tossed her head, realizing as she did that a good part of her hair had worked its way free of her caged headdress and was visible for every living soul at Windsor Castle to gape at. "I truly have no idea," she said loftily. "I suppose you couldn't help me with my hair, could you?"

Gilbert snorted. "I'm not a lady's maid. And after that display, who will notice?" He continued dragging her through the crowd until he finally reached its fringes. "Christ, I don't see Hugh anywhere in this mob. Half of England must be here. Do you know where you were lodged?"

"It had a lovely view of the river. With the leaves off the trees you can look right out of it and see all the comings and goings there. I even saw the sun set today, Gilbert." She sighed. "It was beautiful."

Despite his piratical appearance, Gilbert was usually quite good-natured, but tonight he was unaccountably grumpy, Bess thought. When she told him so, he muttered something that Bess could not make out, but which was probably most unchivalrous, and settled her on a bench aside the wall. "Stay here. I'm going to look for Hugh or your father or one of your brothers to take you to your chamber. Or at least I can find the king's steward to tell me where it is and I can take you there myself. Don't you dare have another drink while I'm gone, and don't you move. Understand? Just rest here and think of your sunset. And for

God's sake stay away from the king. He's almost as flown by wine as you are, which is saying something. Understand? Not even a sip!"

Glad to be sitting for the moment, Bess nodded and dreamily watched him hurry off. Then she started. Her father! He would be so angry at her, making a display of herself and even flirting with the king a little. And her mother would be even worse. Bess blanched at the very thought. Best that she go to her chamber in dignity now instead of waiting to be hauled there in disgrace. She had a fairly good idea of where it was and could have led Gilbert straight to it, if only he hadn't stormed off in such a huff.

She lurched to her feet, deciding to ignore the sound of the train of her gown ripping as she did, and made her way out of the hall, supporting herself against the wall when needed. As she passed a window seat she stumbled over a couple embracing there. Joan of Kent and Sir Thomas Holland? Surely it could not be; the wine must be playing more tricks with her. She ignored them, as she had the rip, and continued on her way, teetering through vaguely familiar passages and up and down likely staircases until she finally saw what had to be her door and pushed her body against it. It did not give.

Bess stared at the upstart door indignantly. She was beginning to beat it with her fists when a voice called, "Bess?"

"Hugh!" She turned, lost her balance, and would have fallen if Hugh had not hastened up the stairs and grabbed her. She said crossly, "I have looked everywhere for you. Where have you been?"

"Looking for you," said Hugh. "Didn't Gilbert tell you to stay where you were?"

Bess suddenly plopped down on the step on which she was standing. "Yes, but he was really quite rude about it, and I hate rude men. He wouldn't even help me with my hair. Oh, sit down, Hugh." He obeyed and she leaned against him contentedly, all her worries gone now that he and not her father had found her. "It was such a nice feast for us ladies. There was porpoise, and salmon, and venison, and—oh, I don't know what all. Oh, and there was the most excellent wine."

"So I understand."

"Well, of course, there is always wine at court. But tonight there was wine from everywhere. We tried all sorts." Bess frowned, then giggled. "Joan had far too much."

"Did she, now?"

"Oh, yes. And I had a little more than usual myself, I think, Hugh. To be quite honest."

"I think so, too. Enough to float you down the Thames to London and back, I'd say."

"Silly, who would want to do that?" She moved into Hugh's lap and began caressing his cheek. "Maybe a little more than usual. Hugh? I did see something very strange. Joan was kissing Sir Thomas Holland." She decided not to mention the king's kissing her own self. "You haven't kissed other women tonight, have you, Hugh?"

"No. Come. Let's get you to our chamber and put you to bed." He tried to haul her to her feet.

"But it's locked, Hugh. And everything goes round when I stand up. It's so much nicer sitting here. Don't you think so?" Bess settled back into Hugh's lap and kissed him. "I liked the king's feast, but I wish you had been there." She began fumbling with his clothing. "Maybe we should go inside after all," she whispered. "We can drink some more wine and dance together and make love."

"Bess, we're not—"

"A bit late for petitioners, Sir Hugh, is it not? Not that I am accustomed to such visits anyway."

Hugh clapped a hand over Bess's mouth as the dowager queen, trailed by her ladies and accompanied by a page or two, stared down at them. "I beg your pardon, your grace. Lady Despenser is not familiar with the layout here. She got confused and took the wrong direction."

His hand slipped and Bess said obstinately, "I did not." She clutched Hugh tighter. "Make them go away, Hugh. I want to be all alone with you. I don't want them coming in our chamber. It's too late for guests."

"All right, Bess." Hugh stood, bowed as best he could to Isabella, and after considering for a moment hauled a protesting Bess over his shoulder like a sack of grain. "Good night, your grace."

"YOU WERE FURIOUS," Hugh said cheerfully, laying a cold towel on Bess's forehead. Bess appreciated the towel, but not her husband's good cheer, so she scowled and said not a word of thanks. "The dowager queen had no business turning us out of our own chambers, you kept telling me, and I kept telling you that you'd taken the wrong turn and were headed toward *her* chambers. But you wouldn't have any of it. You're a mulish little thing with too much wine in you, sweetheart; it's damn lucky you weren't born a man or you'd probably have had your head broken a dozen times over by now. Anyway, I finally got you undressed and in bed—your poor ladies couldn't have managed it. At that point you stopped being angry at me for taking the queen's part and became insistent on being ravished. You were quite the wanton. That bearskin by the fire may bring back some memories if you think hard enough."

Bess gazed bleakly at the bearskin. It, like its former occupant, had seen better days, probably several King Edwards ago. "And then?"

"Oh, you wanted more wine, of course, but I wouldn't give it to you. You wanted to dance too, but I wouldn't. You sulked for a little while about that; it was almost like the old days of our marriage. Poor Bess, I wager you've a head on you today. If it's any consolation, you're very far from being the only lady so afflicted, I hear."

"I hate the king. How dare he give us so much wine?"

She struggled to a sitting position. Hugh, naturally, had been unable to braid her hair for her the night before, and the very weight of it hanging loose made her wince as she slowly arose.

Seeing that Hugh was fully dressed, she asked, "Hugh, where are you going?"

"It's time for dinner. So I'm going to"—Bess with a great effort managed to get out of bed and hasten in the direction of the garderobe—"dinner. Did I say the wrong word, sweetheart?"

AFTER SEVERAL TRIPS to the garderobe, Bess went back to bed and slept, opening her eyes only when Hugh returned to their chamber. "How was—dinner?" she asked, relieved that the word no longer gave her palpitations

"Very pleasant. I danced with Queen Philippa and she called me delectable and I gave her a great smacking kiss right in front of the whole nobility of England. One of your sisters was there to protect my virtue, fortunately."

She sat up. "Hugh, I meant to tell you—"

"So you do remember? I was thinking that your memory was strangely weak on who was kissing whom last night."

"Gilbert must have—"

"Gilbert told me only that you'd had too much to drink and were acting rather foolishly. He didn't tell me that you'd all but invited the king into your bed. That I've heard from others, all of this afternoon."

"Hugh! I wouldn't have known the king from the Pope at the time."

"Well, that raises an even more interesting picture, though certainly not a more pleasing one. In any case, we can discuss this later, as I've an invitation for you that you need to attend to now. Not from the king, you might be distressed to hear—"

"Hugh!"

"—and not from the Pope either, by the way. I don't think you'd be able to guess if you tried, even if you could try in your present state. The she-wolf herself, otherwise known as our gracious lady the king's mother."

Bess frowned, a painful process. "Queen Isabella? What on earth does she want with me?"

Hugh shrugged. "Maybe she wants to apologize for turning you out of your chambers last night. She'll probably offer you excellent wine, if my memory from when I was a squire at court serves me right."

"Hugh—"

"I'll call in your ladies. They've got a lot to work to do on you, my dear."

ESCHEWING THE ELABORATE GOWNS she had had made for her visit to court, Bess ordered that her ladies dress her in an older traveling gown that made her look as frumpy and matronly as she could at her age. Arranging her hair into her customary headdress would have been far too painful, and brought back faintly distasteful memories besides, so she settled for a simple veil and wimple and proceeded toward the dowager queen's chamber. Her sister-in-law, Joan of Kent, was hobbling up one flight of stairs as Bess hobbled down them. "Joan? Are you all right?"

"I wish I were on my deathbed."

"So do I."

Even Joan of Kent's beauty, Bess observed with muted pleasure, did not hold up well under a massive hangover. And had she really seen Joan with Thomas Holland? Given Bess's own conduct with the king, not to mention whatever sinful act she must have instigated on the bearskin rug, she supposed that she was not in a position to be censorious.

Joan was not so bleary-eyed, however, as to miss Bess's voluminous wimple, the sort that was no longer seen in fashionable company except on nuns and ladies over sixty. "What in the name of God is that on your head?"

"Go to the devil, Joan," said Bess, thinking that their conversation had taken a peculiarly circular turn.

The ornate entrance to Queen Isabella's apartments was so different from the simple one to hers and Hugh's that no sober person could have mistaken the two. A page showed her in, and Bess sank to a curtsey, though every bone she had resisted. She spoke the words that she had been rehearsing since Hugh had given her the news. "Your grace, I beg your pardon for my inexcusable and disgraceful behavior last night. I assure you it shall never happen again."

"Inexcusable and disgraceful? Ridiculous will do, Lady Despenser." The queen waved her to a stool. "Sit there. You brought some needlework with you, I see? Show it to me."

"It is for our portable altar, your grace."

"Very pretty. You work very nicely. Don't look so frightened, child. I didn't call you here to upbraid you. So you are wondering, no doubt, what did I call you here for?"

"My head aches so badly, your grace, I could hardly figure it out if I tried."

Isabella laughed. "Well, it's no mystery, Lady Despenser. You are the eldest daughter of my son's favorite earl and wife to one of the wealthiest men in England. It would be remiss of me not to take some notice of you." She settled back with her own work. "I gather you haven't been to court much."

"No, your grace. I have mostly stayed on my father's lands and now my husband's."

"And you have visited your husband's aunt, Lady Elizabeth de Burgh. She is an old friend of mine. She has spoken very highly of you."

"There were no opportunities for me to make a fool out of myself when I visited her. I suppose that is why."

Isabella chuckled. "She said you were a clever girl. So was I, at your age. I noticed you and your pretty sister-in-law looking at me quite intently last night."

Bess blushed. "We did not mean to be rude. It is just that your grace is so handsome, and the king's mother, and so seldom seen, and—"

"A wicked woman, I am sure you have been told. I suppose if I were a young lady again I would stare at me too." She paused. "Don't fear, Lady Despenser. I won't force you to turn confessor. I have a perfectly good one of my own."

Relieved and disappointed at the same time, Bess concentrated on her needlework. To break the silence, she said, "If it is not being impertinent, is it strange being back at court after all this time?"

"Why should a girl who embraces her king in front of a hall of people worry about being impertinent? I miss very little, you see."

"Your grace——"

"Oh, I blame my son entirely. He shouldn't have filled the hall with ladies, half of them who have never been outside their little shires before, brought out his best wines, and not expected half of them to make fools of themselves. My husband had the right idea. He discouraged women from being at court, unless they were among my ladies and damsels."

She spoke of her husband as if she were an ordinary widow, Bess noted with fascination.

"In any case, to answer your question, it is very strange being back at court. It is full of ghosts. No, my child, I'm not addled in the head. I mean the ghosts of men and women who live in their children. My son is the living image of his father as a young man, although they're not the same in character. Your husband is another such one as to his wicked father. My granddaughter Isabella could have been me when I first came to England, they all say. And I could think of a dozen other examples. Yet all these ghosts are wandering around in a very different world than the one in which I lived. And none of them seem to know what to make of me. Fortunately, I still have some friends who have aged with me."

The dowager queen studied her work for a moment or two. "I spoke just now of your husband. I have known him since he was a small boy, though last night was probably the first time we have spoken in twenty years. Is he good to you?"

"Very good, your grace." She batted back a tear.

"I daresay he is or you would have been beaten black and blue last night. Of course, his father treated his mother well too, and he was a blackguard. So that proves very little, I suppose."

"He is a good man, your grace, and not just to me."

"Aye? I once wanted him dead, you know. Too dangerous to have him alive, I thought, and I can't say it was unpleasant thinking of him dead either, not with that father of his. But he held out in that castle long enough to allow me to change my mind and to let him live. And the king didn't want to execute him either, him being his cousin. He was lucky."

"No," said Bess. "He was brave."

"Brave, but lucky too. He could have been executed straight-away like his father, or if he had been let out after a few months as that mother of his requested, God knows what sort of treason he might have got up to. He might have ended up dead with the Earl of Kent. I assume that you are close to your sister-in-law Joan, then?"

"Yes. We spent much time in the same household while growing up."

"Does she ever speak of her father?"

Bess decided not to mention Joan's remark about Isabella killing her father. "Very seldom, your grace. She was such a child when he died, she never knew him, really."

"No. His death is something I do regret."

Bess hardly heard the words, they were spoken in such an undertone. The dowager queen continued, "Well, as far as your Hugh goes, I bear him no ill will. He has served my son the king loyally. Some might have borne a grudge in his circumstances, or simply sulked, and I have to give him credit for not doing so. Perhaps you can tell him someday that I wish him nothing but well. I have sometimes thought of doing so myself, but it would probably be an unpleasant experience for both of us. Too much happened for us to ever want to meet more than superficially. Last night was quite enough for me and for him as well, I dare-say."

"I will tell him, your grace."

"Good. Seeing him last night put me in mind of what I had left unsaid. It was probably the true reason I asked you here, as a matter of fact. I thought I should say it now, for I don't know when we shall meet again after these festivities are over. My son the king does not force me to live on my lands, as I have heard ill-informed people say, but I find that it is better for all concerned that I spend most of my time on them. Queen Philippa is very gracious, but I suspect I make her uneasy. Her and all the younger women here."

"Your grace—"

"There is no need to lie to make me feel better, child. As I said earlier, I can't blame them, or you. And it is uncomfortable for me too. I envy all of you innocent girls, with your simple lives. It reminds me of what I lost through my own stupidity. And my stupidity was great indeed, for I am not naturally a stupid woman." She gazed at Bess severely. "I trust this confidence shall not be the talk of the court tomorrow?"

"Of course not, your grace," said Bess, a little hurt.

"Good. I never thought it would be—your father is an honorable man, and I suppose he imbued it in you—but one never knows. In any case, I have had my say." She gazed at Bess again, this time appraisingly. "They will be holding the tournament soon, so we must be getting ready. I do hope your husband is not mean with all of his money? For that dress and wimple are fit only for a soggy day in Wales, Lady Despenser."

WHEN BESS RETURNED TO HER CHAMBER, Hugh and one of his clerks were working on some of his correspondence to and from his estates. She listened to him as he finished dictating a letter. His voice was listless, and twice he had to go back and amend what he had just said. "Hugh, can I see you alone?"

The clerk looked relieved. Hugh shrugged. "Might as well. Nothing much is getting accomplished at the moment." He waited until the clerk left. "Well?"

She sat down. "You're not at the tournament," she said lamely, though it was not much of a surprise. Hugh had grown up at the court of the second Edward, who had discouraged tournaments, and at the time when they had been revived by Mortimer and Isabella, he had of course been imprisoned. Once he had been freed, it had taken a while for him to feel welcome in the lists. Though he now acquitted himself reasonably well on the tournament field, he'd never developed the passion for jousting that the king and others had.

"I had some business to attend to here, and I'm not to take part today anyway. Tomorrow, I think. Is that what you wanted me to clear the room to ask?"

"No. The queen told me that she once wanted you dead."

He shrugged. "No surprise there."

"Hugh, that would have been terrible!" In spite of Hugh's inhospitable look, she perched herself on his lap and put her arms around him protectively.

"Well, you wouldn't have been around to know," Hugh said. She frowned and held him more tightly. His voice softened. "Why, Bess, I think you've grown to like me after all."

"A bit." Even as she attempted to banter with him, she felt tears begin to come to her eyes. "Hugh, last night with the king meant nothing! Nothing! I was so addled, and thinking that I was beautiful and witty, that is all. I would never be unfaithful to you. I would never even think of it. I can't bear to have you suppose that I am that type of woman. I did not mean to shame you."

"Bess, I know. I was harsh earlier. It'd been tedious, with my friends telling me that you couldn't possibly have meant any harm and everyone else speculating on when and with whom you would cuckold me if you hadn't already."

"Oh, Hugh."

"But you need to be more careful from here on, everywhere and not just with the king. You're not a child, you're a lovely woman. It's not hard to lead a man where he's tempted to go anyway, sweetheart. Being a man, and having been tempted myself, I speak with the best of authority on the subject."

"Hugh, I am so sorry."

He shrugged. "It'll be forgotten by tomorrow. There will more feasting tonight, and I'm sure there will be enough making fools of themselves to supply plenty of fodder for the gossips in the morning."

"Not I. Does Papa know? And Mama?"

"I haven't seen your mother, but your father spoke to me in private. I told him that it was nothing, just a silly drunken dare between you and Joan of Kent. He nodded and said that you and Joan had gotten into scrapes before and he wasn't at all surprised. He's got something else on his mind, anyway. Some grand idea of the king's of which he won't say a word."

"Thank you, Hugh." She rested her still-throbbing head against his shoulder.

He stroked her cheek. "Truth is," he admitted. "I didn't go to the tournament because I was hoping you would come back here."

"I am so glad that I did."

"So what else did the dowager queen say to you?"

"She was quite civil to me, Hugh, and she gave me a message to you." She told Hugh of their conversation.

Hugh smiled ruefully. "Well, I'm glad the she-wolf has a conscience. I've tried to put aside my own hate for her, and I like to think I succeeded some time ago. If not, perhaps I can now." He glanced outside the window. "Shall we go to the tournament now? I know you haven't been to many of them."

"No." She put her lips to his and slid a little forward on his lap, feeling his reaction as she did so. She kissed him lazily as his hands began to rove. "Do you know what else the queen told me? That my dress was dowdy."

"Then by all means let's get you out of it."

Their lovemaking was much the same as usual: easy, gentle, and loving, though perhaps with a certain edge that had been missing before, Bess thought. "Better than the tournament?" Hugh asked as they lay in each other's arms afterward. They could hear it in the background, a gentle rumble.

"Much better. But— Hugh?"

"Sweetheart?"

"What did happen on that mangy-looking rug? Was it *very* sinful?"

Hugh laughed. "Bess, sweetheart, I was teasing you. You did arrange yourself on the rug, most fetchingly. Then you fell fast asleep; it's a wonder you weren't out long before that. I picked you up and carried you to bed. Nothing you have to trouble your confessor with, I promise."

Still, Bess thought, she would have any bear rugs on their estates destroyed straightaway.

AT THE END OF THE THREE DAYS OF JOUSTING, the ladies awarded six prizes, three going to the king, who all agreed deserved them. Bess was pleased to see that Hugh's cousin, Philip le Despenser, the only son of his father's long-dead brother, won one of the remaining prizes.

With the jousts seemingly over, Bess thought the festivities would soon be breaking up, but the king, it appeared, had other thoughts in mind. In a booming voice, he announced that the company was to remain at Windsor and that all were to assemble the next morning near the chapel, where he planned to make a great announcement. Bess was not overly enthusiastic to hear this news, for after her giddy first evening at Windsor, she had soon wearied of the feasting and jousts, especially since she had taken a cue from her mother and learned to get through a seemingly endless night of revelry on a couple of cups of heavily watered wine. Now she was eager to get back to her own estates, to ride around in her everyday dress and see how the tenants were faring and to admire the new babies, animal and human, that had been born in her absence. Nonetheless, she was as curious as anyone else about what the king would have to say. Surely nothing that would send Hugh away from her again, she prayed.

Since her foolish display several nights before, Bess had scarcely looked at the king. Now as the king came out of the chapel where he had been hearing mass, Bess could not take her eyes off him, nor could anyone else. He might have been going to his own coronation, Bess thought, so splendid were his velvet robes. Behind him walked Queen Philippa, heading toward stoutness but tall enough that she still could carry off her own splendid garments; Queen Isabella, dressed so as not to outshine the younger queen but somehow managing to give the impression that she could certainly still do so if she pleased; thirteen-year-old Edward, made Prince of Wales the year before; Henry of Grosmont, assuming the role of steward of England in the stead of his aged, blind father, Henry of Lancaster; and the king's earl marshal, Bess's own father. Bess's eyes misted with tears of pride as William de Montacute took his place by a huge book on which the king laid his hand. Not until now had she fully grasped how high her father was in the king's favor.

"God has given England much success in these past years, but there is still much to be done," the king said. "To do this we must be as one. We look around us today and we are well pleased at what we see—the finest and best knights in England, and the fairest group of ladies ever to be assembled in one place. We look around us, and we are reminded of the glorious days of King Arthur himself.

"With that in mind, it is our intent to begin a Round Table in the same manner as the great King Arthur appointed it, to the number of three hundred knights, always increasing. It is our intention to cherish and maintain it according to our power. We shall erect a building here at Windsor just for that purpose, and we shall meet there every year. We take this vow today, on these Holy Gospels!"

The crowd cheered wildly as Edward took the solemn oath, followed by his steward and the earl marshal and four other earls. Then, with an exuberant sound of trumpets, yet another feast began, this one surpassing all of the rest.

BESS STOOD ON THE LADIES' PLATFORM as yet another round of jousting began, the king having decided that more was required in order to celebrate the announcement of the Round Table. The day was chillier than the preceding ones had been, and she was grateful that her mantle was amply trimmed with fur inside and out. Indeed, only Queen Philippa, Queen Isabella, and the Lady Isabella wore cloaks richer than Bess's. Bess hoped that the dowager queen, seated some distance away, had duly noted this. Hugh mean, indeed!

She watched the jousting without paying much attention to it, thinking her own thoughts so that the time passed quite quickly. Only when Hugh rode out did she turn her mind as well as her eyes to the jousting. Admiring Hugh's bright red-and-gold surcoat and horse trappings, emblazoned with his arms and looking even brighter against skies that looked as if they could snow any minute, Bess wondered what Queen Isabella was thinking of all of this fine display of Despenser heraldry. Presumably she was bearing it graciously, for no gasps of horror came from the area in the stands given over to the royal ladies.

Hugh unhorsed his opponent handily. Bess blew a kiss to him and cheered, remained politely attentive as Hugh de Hastings, Hugh's cousin, took his turn, and then became fully attentive once more as her father rode out. Like his king, Bess's father loved to joust, though his forty-three years were beginning to show when he was matched against a younger man.

The two horses rumbled toward each other, gaining speed. The men's lances barely touched. The second turn ended in the same result. The third turn, and William de Montacute was knocked to the ground. Bess groaned in disappointment, along with many other ladies; the handsome Earl of Salisbury was always a favorite in the stands. She watched calmly as her father's squires bent to help their master to his feet, just as so many other squires had done before in this tournament. Then a single word cracked in the air. "Surgeon!"

Bess gathered up her skirts and hurled herself down the steps of the platform, pushing aside all who stood in her path. In front of her, her mother was making the same mad rush down from the lower, more spacious platform where the countesses had taken their places. By the time the Montacute women reached the field, the king's surgeon was bending over her father, joined by her brother and surrounded by a group of knights.

Hugh, who had been in the midst of having his armor removed and was now wearing only his shirt and hose, guided the countess toward the inner circle, then reached for Bess. "Is he dead?" she whispered.

"No."

"Will he die?"

He held her close to him. "I don't know, Bess. Sometimes a man can fall as he did and be up and about moments later with nothing amiss. Sometimes—"

Bess closed her eyes, hoping that when she opened them again her father would be standing up, laughing at the fuss over him. Instead, she fell to the ground. When she next opened her eyes, she was in Hugh's arms, being carried into Windsor Castle.

HER FATHER REMAINED MOSTLY UNCONSCIOUS for days, only occasionally opening his eyes to stare about him and mumble confusedly. Bess, her sisters, and Joan of Kent took turns sitting with him along with the Countess of Salisbury, who almost never left. Bess herself would have stayed all the time were it not for Hugh, who made her walk outside from time to time, though he took care to keep her away from the tournaments that were still going on as if nothing had ever happened.

The king had visited frequently at first, sitting silently by the bedside for hours at a time. His visits became less frequent as the days dragged on, and toward the end of the month Edward left Windsor altogether. Bess told Hugh that she thought that this was callous of him, but Hugh shook his head. "No, Bess. He just can't bear it."

As if she and the other Montacute women could.

As the alternative was pacing the room, she had brought her work with her and kept her hands busy and her mind as calm as she could by sewing a shirt for Hugh or even embroidering while her father lay still and silent next to her. On January 30, having persuaded her mother to lie down in her own chamber, she was concentrating on getting the wings of a lovebird just right when she heard her father whisper, "Bess."

"Papa!" She bent and kissed him. "You are better."

"No, Bess." He tried to raise his head but could not. "You'd best get the others."

She nodded to a servant; one was always standing nearby. "Someone is, Papa."

"And a priest." Her father closed his eyes, and for a moment Bess thought he had drifted off into unconsciousness again, or worse. Then he whispered, "Happy, Bess?"

She barely heard the words. "Yes, Papa."

"I was . . . worried . . . few days ago. Hugh . . . so much older. You and Ed—"

She could have broken down and cried. "No, Papa. I was being foolish. I love Hugh very much. You chose well for me. And I thank you from the bottom of my heart." Bess hesitated, then came out with her lie. What would such a small sin matter to the Lord if it brought some cheer to her dying father? "I am not sure, Papa, but I think I am carrying Hugh's child. Your first grandchild."

He smiled. "Good girl." Then he frowned again. "Will . . . pretty Joan. Something . . . wrong there. I think."

"They are very young still, Papa. They will work it out. I promise."

Her father sighed and was quiet for a while. "Prosper, my little Bess," he whispered finally. "Bess. Promise me . . ."

"Anything, Papa. Anything."

"Tell your children . . . the story. Nottingham." Weak as he was, his smile was a triumphant one, wide enough to include the rest of the family and the priest who had hurried into the room. "'Tis a good one, lass, isn't it?"

November 1346 to August 1347

In her chamber at Hanley Castle, Bess smoothed out a sheet of parchment, written in Hugh's own unpracticed hand. It had been written that previous summer aboard ship. Even now, Bess thought, a pleasantly salty smell clung to it. Hugh had apparently had trouble getting started on this letter that he evidently had deemed too personal to dictate to a clerk, for several lines had been scratched over. Bess after some effort had been able to make them out:

> *My dear and esteemed wife. I hope the receipt of this letter finds you well. I am in good health, and so are all of the men with me thus far.*

> *I regret that the French have brought us to this pass, and even more I regret the separation from you that this entails. But we all pray that right will prevail and that victory will be ours.*

> *You are so lovely. I could kiss your*

> *I know that you will take excellent care of the estates while I am away. All of my men are trustworthy, so I have no worries on that score.*

Finally, Hugh had found words to his satisfaction:

It was much easier to part in 1342 when we were both angry with each other, wasn't it, sweet Bess? I love you. God be with you, and if He is good, we shall be together again. If it turns out that we must part forever, know that you have always been my dearest love.

I miss you, sweetheart.

Hugh.

She unfolded a second parchment, which was a copy that Bess's own clerk had made for her from one that was making the rounds throughout England. She skimmed it, knowing by now exactly where the parts of the most interest to her could be found. Sir Hugh le Despenser, along with the Earl of Suffolk, killing two hundred or more commoners who had taken up arms near Poix. The Earl of Northampton, Reginald Cobham, and Sir Hugh le Despenser leading the king's troops across the River Somme, scattering the enemy awaiting them on the other side and even in the water. Sir Hugh le Despenser and his men taking and burning the towns of Noyelles-sur-Mer and Le Crotoy, killing four hundred men-at-arms in the latter town. Sir Hugh le Despenser leading part of the rearguard when in August, at a place called Crécy, the English troops, sorely outnumbered, had won a stunning victory over the French. And now the English army was besieging Calais.

Folding the parchments neatly, Bess slipped them back into the Book of Hours in which she treasured them, then went to the castle chapel to pray for the safety of Hugh and his men, Emma's husband among them. When she returned, a messenger was waiting with a letter from the constable at Cardiff Castle. It regarded provisions for Hugh's French prisoners, a number of whom were being lodged quite comfortably by Bess in Wales. They were too flirtatious to keep with her at Hanley, she'd decided.

Bess was dictating a reply when Emma, who'd come to visit that morning and was sitting beside her sewing a garment for the second child she would soon be having, went to the window. "Another messenger is riding up! This one in royal livery. Shall we go to the hall?"

"No." If there was bad news, she wanted to face it in the privacy of her own chamber, not in a hall full of people preparing for dinner. She remained where she was, drumming her fingers of her right hand against her left wrist and looking around at her surroundings. Like that of many an English lady, her chamber might as well have been in the heart of Paris, filled as it was with booty that was already being shipped back from the French campaign. Emma's more modest chamber at her own manor was scarcely less Frenchified, there having been plenty of treasure to go around.

In a few minutes, the knock came and the messenger, who to Bess's relief did not look particularly solemn, bowed before her. Handing her the parchment, he said, "My lady, I've delivered several of these today. The ladies have been enjoying them."

Bess nearly snatched it from his hand to read it. Then she let out a whoop, embraced the messenger, and kissed him soundly on the cheek. "Reward him for his pains and give him our best ale," she told her servant, trying to recover some dignity. Giving up the effort, she embraced Emma.

"I gather the news is good. My lord is coming home?"

Bess shook her head. "No—he is staying in Calais. But the news is good. We—I and the queen and her daughters and many others—are going there!"

SO MANY LADIES had been invited to go to Calais that an apprehensive Frenchman could have taken their fleet for that of a second wave of invaders. Bess's mother, who'd taken a vow of chastity after her husband's death, had stayed behind, but the Montacute women were amply represented by Bess, Sybil, and Philippa, all of whom had husbands in Calais. Sybil had married Hugh's nephew Edmund Arundel, while Philippa—much to

Hugh's amusement—had married the grandson of the wicked Roger Mortimer. "Montacutes, Mortimers, and Despensers all at one table next Twelfth Night, perhaps. Who'd had thought it possible?"

Joan of Kent was there, as was Hugh's sister Isabel, the former Countess of Arundel, whose husband had finally succeeded in having their marriage annulled. Isabel had gone not only to see her son and her brothers, she admitted to Bess cheerily, but also to discomfit the new Countess of Arundel, a cousin of Isabel's whom the earl had married with unbecoming haste after the Pope had issued the annulment. In this Isabel had succeeded, for the new countess had looked anything but pleased as her predecessor arrived at Dover Castle, dressed in finery provided by Hugh's generosity and hardly looking the part of a cast-off wife whose son had been declared a bastard.

Their voyage having been a surprisingly smooth one, the ladies were all on deck and all dressed in their finest clothes as the harbor of Calais came into view. Though the queen was an old hand at making the journey across the Channel, most of the other ladies had never crossed before, and fewer still had been present at a siege. Eager as she was to see her husband, Bess half dreaded getting off the cog. Would the shore be littered with corpses? Would the stink of death be everywhere? And where on earth would she sleep?

The harbor, however, looked quiet, although as the ship came closer Bess could see that it was heavily guarded to keep out enemy vessels. She impatiently awaited her turn to be rowed to shore. Each small boat full of ladies was being watched anxiously by a cluster of men, and each time a knight was reunited with his lady, a cheer went up from the troops.

A boat came back to the ship, was filled with ladies, and made the journey to shore and back with excruciating slowness. Then Bess, her sisters, and Hugh's sister were finally assisted into a boat, rowed by the slowest oarsmen in Christendom, Bess decided. At last a man offered her his hand and assisted her out of the boat. "Hugh!"

A cheer went up as they embraced. Somehow Hugh moved her out of the way of the others disembarking; she knew not how, for she had not left his arms.

THE QUEEN HAVING LANDED well before the others and having ridden on horseback to the English camp, the remaining ladies and their men were following on foot, not unhappily, for it gave them more precious time together. "I have heard the reports about you, Hugh. The crossing of the Somme, and Le Crotoy—"

He grinned. "Aye, something to regale the nephews with at last. They were beginning to find my Scottish tales a bit dull."

"You will tell me about them too?"

"Certainly, my love." He glanced around to see who was within earshot. "But only after I've had my way with you."

She giggled. "Are we to live in a tent? I daresay I can get used to it—but lying together in your tent with your squires within arm's reach?"

"Only my most discreet squires."

"Hugh!"

"I think you'll find that we've arranged things nicely."

Bess had her doubts, but she put them aside and took in the sight of Hugh again. As always after he had been fighting for a while, he was leaner and more taut, with a face browned from the sun. He and the other men had had adequate warning of the ladies' arrival, however, for all seemed fresh from their barbers, with neatly trimmed hair and beards. She began to wish herself nearer to their living quarters too, whatever they might be.

Nearby, Sybil, walking hand in hand with Edmund, gasped. Bess turned her attention from her husband's attractions to the direction of her sister's stare. Then she let out a gasp that rivaled Sybil's.

Outside the walls of Calais, a miniature city of wood had sprouted. Streets, perfectly symmetrical and lined with look-alike houses and shops of timber, intersected with other streets, surrounding a market square. One wooden building, bigger than any of the others, bore Edward's arms. From several long structures came the sound of neighing. On the fringes, precariously near the shore, were rows upon rows of huts.

"The king has named it Villeneuve-le-hardie," said Hugh. "See that house near the square? That's mine—ours."

But Bess was too enchanted with the town to care much about her own house. It was almost like a toy, she thought. "Why, it even has taverns!"

"Aye, but you'd best not go inside that one, sweetheart. Food isn't the main concern there."

She followed his eye and saw a pair of women, heads uncovered and wearing dresses that did little to conceal the contours of their voluptuous figures. "Hugh! I hope you have not—"

He grinned. "No, sweetheart, but they're part of the reason you're here. The king thought we could use some more civilized company. And he's a wise man. We could."

"The queen was on another ship, of course, so we were all speculating as to why the king summoned us. What's the other part of the reason?"

"He has a wedding in mind, it seems. The Lady Isabella to Louis, the new Count of Flanders. Louis doesn't have much choice in the matter, it appears; he's only sixteen, and he's all but controlled by his people instead of the other way around. To make matters worse, the old count was slain at Crécy, before the son's eyes, so I'm not sure this bodes well for the proposed match. But we shall see."

Bess had met the Lady Isabella, the king's eldest daughter, at Windsor. Isabella had been only twelve then, but she already possessed a considerable sense of her own worth, Bess had thought at the time. Even in happier circumstances, Louis was likely to find the marriage a trying one, she suspected. "When is it to take place?"

"No time soon; I don't think the king has even opened negotiations yet. But enough about this. Here is the Maison le Despenser!"

She giggled as Hugh lifted her and carried her across the threshold; up and down the street, other knights were doing the same with their ladies. When he kissed her and set her down, she looked around. She was standing in a miniature hall, backing up to a miniature kitchen. Upstairs, she discovered when Hugh guided her to a staircase, was a large bedchamber, obviously Hugh's, and a couple of smaller ones, where Bess supposed that some of Hugh's men slept. "It is like a house for a doll," she said.

"I'm afraid you'll find it cramped after a while, but we're hoping the French king will see reason soon and end this."

She looked outside. "I have never been in a siege before. I thought it would be more—warlike. All I hear is hammering from the king's works."

"This is the quiet type of siege. We're starving them out."

Bess had heard of such sieges, but she had never had to consider the matter so closely. She winced as the smell of cooking drifted up the staircase. Seeing her face change, Hugh said, "I'd prefer not to see them starve either, but there's no other way to take the town; its natural defenses won't allow it. The poorest citizens were made to leave not long ago, so there'd be less mouths to feed. Our king gave them a meal and a safe passage through our troops."

"How long do you think it will last?"

"That's entirely up to the French king. But haven't we had enough war talk for now?" He grinned and led Bess to the bed, which was small but proved to be entirely serviceable for the purpose to which the couple put it.

THE WEEKS SLIPPED INTO MONTHS as the siege dragged on. Most of the ladies returned to England after the Yuletide festivities, but the queen and the Lady Isabella stayed behind, as did most of the wives of the king's commanders.

With the population of Calais starving within sight, Bess felt wretchedly guilty for her own small privation, boredom. Yet bored she was. Used to riding around Hugh's sprawling estates and directing a large household, she had nowhere to go now except into the market square or to the homes of the other wives, and the ridiculously small staff it took to run the Calais house hardly needed direction. She eagerly watched the harbor for English ships, anxious to get whatever messages had been sent from her and Hugh's estates, but the messages when they arrived were usually of the dullest sort. Hugh's experienced stewards had matters at home well in hand, it seemed. The only news of interest came from Emma: she had borne a healthy girl, named Elizabeth after Bess.

The men in Calais were busier than the women. The English had not yet succeeded in blocking all access to the port, and occasionally a ship laden with supplies for the townspeople of Calais would slip through. From time to time the king tried to assault the town's walls, without success, and occasionally someone would head inland on a foraging raid. Still, Hugh spent most nights next to Bess in their bed, and seeing him every morning upon waking more than compensated Bess for the tedium of Calais.

Joan of Kent had remained in Calais too, in a house the king had provided for her and Will on account of his affection for his late friend the Earl of Salisbury and on account of Will's having succeeded to his father's earldom. Like Bess, Joan had yet to conceive a child, and this, at least as far as Bess was concerned, had brought the two of them closer together in an outpost where almost all of the other married women were constantly talking of children, those who had been born and those who were on the way. When ships came in bringing new goods from Flanders or even England, Bess and Joan would run to see what was being unloaded, and on the dull days when nothing new was going on in the marketplace, they would go to the building that had been designated as a royal palace and spend the day with Queen Philippa and the rest of the wives. The queen's eldest daughter, the Lady Isabella, was there too, rather to her chagrin, for her intended husband had jilted her, using the pretext of a falconing expedition to get on a fast horse and ride for dear life from Flanders into France. Fortunately, Isabella had taken this in stride; doted on by both parents and with an ample household, she had been in no hurry to exchange her very comfortable life at home for the unknown quantities of a husband, especially a husband who had some cause to bear her homeland ill will. The wives of Calais, who had been hoping for the excitement of a royal wedding to break up the tedium, were the only ones who had seemed truly affected by the broken engagement.

Spring had arrived in Calais, and with it a growing certainty that the people inside the city walls could not withstand the siege much longer, when Bess, coming home from a dull afternoon sewing with the queen, entered her tiny hall and was stopped by a servant. "My lady, your brother the Earl of Salisbury is upstairs with Sir Hugh. He seems—agitated."

Bess hurried upstairs. Was Joan ill? She had not been in Queen Philippa's chambers, though that very morning she and Bess had gone to the marketplace to admire a shipment of fabric from Flanders. Nothing had seemed amiss with Joan then, except that she had had difficulty choosing between a bolt of green and a bolt of blue and had finally settled the matter in an eminently sensible way by purchasing both. "Will! What is the matter?"

Will sat on a stool, his face in his hands. He said nothing. Beside him stood Hugh, looking as ill at ease as Bess had ever seen him in his life. "Hugh! Is it Joan? Is she ill? She was fine this morn—"

"She is not ill." Will lifted his head but stared off into space.

"Will, *talk* to me."

Will made an effort to compose himself. "We had an argument."

"Over what?" Bess prompted when it seemed that her brother was not going to continue.

"Over—who knows? I don't remember—I don't care now. All I know is that it turned into a row. We've had plenty of them. She said she wished she'd never married me. She's said that before too. But this time—"

He broke down in tears. Bess knelt beside her brother and put her arms around him. Never in her life had she seen carefree Will like this. "Will. Please. Tell me. It can't be all that bad."

"Oh, yes, it can be." Will blew his nose. "She said that she's not my true wife at all, that all these years she's been married to Sir Thomas Holland."

Bess rocked back on her heels.

She had passed Sir Thomas Holland that very morning. Though he'd lost an eye on this excursion to France, he was still a handsome man, his eye patch making him look jaunty rather than maimed. Dear Lord, he was Will's own steward! It was not hard to imagine her beautiful sister-in-law flirting with him, but married? Then, dimly, she remembered that night at Windsor Castle where she'd seen him and Joan caressing in a corner. She'd never mentioned it in all these years, thinking that in her inebriation her mind must have been playing tricks on her, but now she recalled every detail perfectly, Joan's leg brushing Holland's; his hand cupping her bosom as he kissed her neck; their groans as they moved closer together, thinking they were unseen in the darkness. She shook her head, as if doing so would erase the memory. Instead, more came to her: Joan's strange behavior at her wedding, her flood of tears when Bess had visited her several years ago, her blithe acceptance of her barrenness that Bess had found so hard to comprehend. She put her arm back on Will's shoulder. "When, Will?"

"When she was twelve, she said. She swears that they married in front of a couple of witnesses, then consummated it that evening. It was not long before Holland went off to Prussia."

"Why did she never mention this to anyone?"

"Damned if I know. I slapped her hard then and walked out." He began to sob again. "I didn't mean to hurt her, Bess."

"Jesus, Will!" She turned to her husband. "I had better go to her, Hugh."

Hugh nodded. "First I'd heard of the slapping part. Will, you'll spend the night here. Bess will talk with Joan. Tomorrow perhaps the two of you can work this out."

He looked highly doubtful, though.

"ARE YOU HERE to beat me too?"

Bess winced when she saw Joan's face. Will had not hit her hard enough to cause a bruise, but she could see a red mark on her cheek. "No, I came to see how you were."

"And to see if I was sharing my bed with Sir Thomas, perhaps."

"Maybe that too," snapped Bess. "Where is he?"

"He's staying with one of his friends."

"A good place for him," said Bess. "Joan, I don't wish to harm you. I only want to understand what has happened. I've never seen Will so miserable, in all my life. Are you truly married to Thomas Holland?"

"I married him when I was twelve, well before I went through that ceremony with your brother."

She made it sound like a pagan rite. Bess held her tongue as her sister-in-law went on. "Sir Thomas knew my mother and your parents wouldn't be happy with the marriage, so we decided he would go off and make his fortune and then claim me. So he went off to Prussia, and while he was still there, it was decided that I should marry your brother."

"So why didn't you say anything?"

"I did, to my mother. I told her that I had an understanding with Sir Thomas. She's not like your parents, Bess. She's highly strung, you know that, and people say she's been like that ever since Papa died. She flew into a rage. She called me a whore and a strumpet and told me that if Sir Thomas came near me she'd have him arrested on whatever grounds she could find or invent. I didn't dare tell her then that I'd given him my maidenhead. I was scared some harm would come to him if anyone found out. So I let them marry me to your brother. He'd never been with a woman, of course, so it was easy to pretend with him that I was still a maid. I yelped and cried a bit. My woman Matilda knew about Sir Thomas and me, so she sprinkled some animal blood on the sheet the next morning to satisfy anyone who cared to inspect it."

"Did you never think of Will in all of this?"

152

Joan ignored the question. "Sir Thomas was gone for so long, I thought that he had forgotten me and everything would work out, except that I loved him and couldn't love Will. But then he did come back, and he found out I was married to Will. He was angry and sad, but he said that it was best that I continue that way, since he didn't have the money to contest the matter and because he didn't wish to hurt my reputation. So we decided to go our separate ways."

"Is that what you were doing when you were making love to him at Windsor Castle?"

Joan's lovely eyes opened wide. "You saw us?" Bess nodded coldly. "I'd had too much to drink and so had he. We were going to our chambers when we met each other outside the hall. We started kissing and then some clumsy oaf fell against us. That brought us to our senses and we parted. But it made us both start thinking that we should be man and wife after all."

"So he took service as Will's steward so he could see you?"

"No! Will asked him; I had nothing to do with it. How could you understand? I've tried to be a good wife to Will, but he's such a boy compared to Tom. And you forget that Tom is my true husband, in the Church's eyes as well as ours. Now that he has his grant for taking that Count d'Eu hostage, he is going to take the case to the papal courts. Then they shall judge me Thomas's wife. I truly believe that is why I have been barren with Will. As a punishment for deserting the man I married."

"Or as a punishment for deceiving Will."

"He's better off marrying elsewhere."

"I certainly believe so, and I hope he does. He deserves better."

Joan shrugged and stood up. "You may leave now, Lady Despenser. Pray tell your brother not to come back here tonight."

HUGH AND BESS'S house was only a few houses down from Joan and Will's. All the houses looked so much alike that coats of arms had had to be nailed to the doors so that their occupants could tell them apart. She walked wearily past the page who opened the Despenser door and went upstairs, where Hugh was waiting in the chamber as though he had never left it. "Where's Will?"

"Sleeping in the next room. He'd had a bit of wine before you came, and he had a bit more after, enough to put him asleep. Good heads for wine don't seem to run in your family." Bess frowned, and he pulled her close to him. "I gather the news from Joan isn't good?"

"She swears that she was married to Thomas Holland when she was twelve and that she was too frightened to tell anyone when they arranged the marriage to Will."

"Poor thing."

"Poor thing! She has humiliated poor Will, shamed our family, and you call her a poor thing!"

Hugh shrugged. "My mother was in a similar fix, did I ever tell you? She and Joan were first cousins; maybe bigamy runs in their family."

"Hugh!" From the next room she heard Will snore. It sounded like an unhappy snore. "How did it happen?"

"God knows. She never said and I never dared to ask; I imagine she was ashamed of herself, poor lady. It wasn't my father, of course, it was Sir William la Zouche and Sir John de Grey, the one of Rotherfield. You've met Grey here, but I guess you didn't know how close he came to having the honor of being my stepfather. Anyway, Zouche and Grey both claimed to have married her. They fought it out for several years in the papal courts, and Grey finally stopped appealing. She was in her thirties when it happened, older and wiser than poor Joan."

"Poor my elbow," muttered Bess.

"While your brother was reasonably sober, I suggested that he send Joan back to England as soon as it can be arranged. No need to say why; he can make the excuse that the situation here disagrees with her health or that he wants her to attend to his estates. Whomever she's married to, she's best off away from both of them until this is settled. It would be awkward if she conceived a child just now. Your brother thought it was a good idea."

"It is, Hugh." A little mollified, she kissed him. "But I think that you are being far too easy on Joan."

"It's Holland who's to blame, sweetheart. He's years older than Joan and should have known better than to get her into this mess. But with a face like that on the girl, what man could help himself?"

Bess's look could freeze over a desert. "Of course, it's a matter of taste, and her looks never appealed that much to— Shall I sleep in the next room with Will, my dear?"

SURPRISINGLY, Joan made no fuss about returning to England, and her excuse of ill health was given credibility by the pale, drawn looks she exhibited on the way to the merchant ship on which she took passage several days later. Bess privately hoped that the ship was boarded by pirates, though she reflected glumly that even they too would likely be bowled over by Joan's heart-shaped face, deep blue eyes, and russet, curling hair. She would probably end up as their queen, with them piling their booty on her lap.

Will, rather to Bess's surprise, had recovered some semblance of his usual good spirits. He rode with Joan to the ship as if nothing amiss were between them, and he kissed her good-bye with affection, though somewhat gingerly. Thomas Holland, wisely, had deeply interested himself in the conduct of the siege that day and was not on hand to bid his bride farewell.

Joan's departure was scarcely commented on by those outside of her immediate family, however, for the siege was in its last gasps. Sickened, Bess had heard the rumors that the citizens of Calais were reduced to eating horseflesh, then that of the few scrawny dogs and cats that still roamed around the town. She had seen a copy of a letter that Jean de Vienne, the governor of Calais, had attempted to smuggle to King Philip. Soon, Jean de Vienne wrote, the men of Calais would be left with the choice between eating each other and walking out into the English lines to face certain death. If Philip did nothing soon, he would not hear from the men of Calais again.

Sent the letter courtesy of King Edward himself, King Philip had reacted by sending an army, camped so close to Calais that its citizens, encouraged, had lit bonfires in celebration. Two peace-making cardinals had arrived as well, but failed utterly in their mission. Then Philip had offered to do battle in a space to be agreed upon between the two sides. It was a battle no one thought the French could win. Since May, fresh English troops had been pouring into the town; the wooden houses of Ville-neuve-le-hardie had long since filled up. Yet Bess waited nervously for word that the site had been chosen. The English had won battles against seemingly impossible odds; so, everyone knew, had the Scots years ago at Bannockburn. What if sheer desperation carried the day and brought victory for the French this time?

She was sleeping after a day of pacing to and fro when Hugh shook her awake at about dawn. "Hugh! You are off to fight?" He shook his head, and she sniffed. "What is burning?"

"Everything the French army couldn't take with them. They've broken camp and left. There will be no battle now; there's no army out there to fight."

"Left! But what of King Philip?"

Hugh shrugged. "No one knows what he was thinking. Maybe he realized that he stood no chance of winning; maybe he thought of giving up Calais to save the rest of France. But he and his men are gone either way, and Jean de Vienne has sued for terms."

"They were brave men to last this long," Bess said hesitantly. "I hope the conditions are not too harsh."

Hugh smiled at her. "Truth is, Bess, I do too. So do most of us, I think."

Yet when the people of Calais offered to surrender, King Edward appeared to be in no mood to offer terms, to the bewilderment of his leaders, who expected that the richest and most prominent citizens would be held to ransom while the others were sent on their way. Edward insisted he would make no promises, but would use the inhabitants of the town in whatever manner he saw fit. All remonstrated with the king, for it was very easy for all of them to imagine themselves at the mercy of their enemies. At last Edward gave in. He would pardon the defenders of Calais their lives—all of them, that was, except for six. With those six he would do as he pleased.

On August 3, 1347, virtually every English person in Calais gathered outside the city walls, King Edward and Queen Philippa on a dais in the middle, flanked by the English earls and the higher-ranking knights like Hugh. Bess and the other English ladies stood in a knot close to the queen. They watched as the gates of Calais slowly opened and Jean de Vienne, emaciated and so weak that he could not walk but had to be put on a horse, rode out, wearing nothing but his shirt, drawers, hose, and a noose around his neck. Behind him, no less emaciated and too weak to take more than slow, uncertain steps, walked five men in identical attire. Only the material of their shirts, worn but still obviously made from a superior cloth, marked them out as being wealthy men. Someone helped Jean de Vienne from his horse, and then all prostrated themselves before Edward. "Have mercy on us, your grace."

The crowd was stark silent as Edward considered the request for a minute or two. "Summon the headsman," he said, and settled back into his chair of state.

The earls and lords on the dais, to a man, began protesting, some of them through tears. Bess herself was weeping, as were the ladies around her, even the Lady Isabella, who was not noted for her sensitive nature. The six men remained prone, praying. Then Queen Philippa rose and descended the platform. She turned to face her husband.

"My lord. I have crossed the seas to be by your side. I have asked very little of you since then. I ask you now to have mercy on these brave men and spare their lives." The queen fell to the ground beside the six men, making seven figures lying in front of the dais.

The crying stopped and the crowd grew silent again. "Very well," said Edward, standing. "Rise, my lady. I cannot refuse what you beg of me so earnestly."

Bess let out the breath she had been holding and felt herself sag with relief. Had the king meant to pardon the men all along? She did not know, and in truth she no longer cared, for she knew now that she and Hugh would soon be going home. Home! As the queen and the six men rose, Bess began smiling.

8

June 1348 to February 1349

The Lady Isabella gave a rare nod of approval. "You make a lovely boy, Bess. If your husband could see you now!"

"Soon he will be seeing me," Bess said glumly. She stared at her hose-covered legs, visible from the knees down. "And what if he recognizes me?"

"You will be masked," said the Lady Isabella patiently.

Bess frowned and touched her hand to her hair beneath the man's cap she was wearing. It was pinned up and hidden under a coif for good measure, but surely when she was on horseback the motion would send it tumbling down. "Hugh will recognize my hair if it falls."

England had been in a giddy mood since Calais had fallen the previous year. With Calais now an English colony, its fine houses occupied by Englishmen and much of its treasure adorning English castles and Englishwomen, the country had been in a mood to celebrate, and the celebrations had yet to stop. Scarcely a month had gone by after one tournament was finished before another was announced. The crowds at each feast and tournament had been more brightly dressed than at the last, the entertainment more outlandish. At the last tournament, a group of unknown ladies, dressed in male clothing, had pranced their horses onto the field, and the sixteen-year-old Lady Isabella had determined to outdo them. To this end, she had enlisted the assistance of her own ladies and that of the younger, more slender wives of the assembled lords and knights. Bess, on the tall side and with especially trim legs, had been a natural for the scheme.

She just hoped Hugh would not be angry at the display she would be making of herself. But she could hardly refuse the king's own eldest daughter, could she?

In any case, she comforted herself, it was not as though the king, at least, were ignorant of what Isabella had in mind. Though Isabella had initially made her plans on a modest scale, arranging to borrow male clothing from her brothers, she had soon discarded this idea in favor of all of the clothing matching, and once this idea was carried out, it would have been unthinkable for the man-ladies to be mounted on anything but matching horses also, with matching trappings. Isabella enjoyed a comfortable income, but this coordination of mounts and materials could not have gone on without the king noticing. Fortunately, he was an indulgent father, especially since his child had been so publicly jilted, and he had given his blessing, and his money, to the show, stipulating only that the cotehardies not be too short and that the women keep on their masks. And so Bess had been conscripted.

It was the sort of display Joan of Kent would have delighted in, but Joan was not at court these days. William was keeping her in strict seclusion on one of the duller Montacute estates while Thomas Holland prosecuted his case to be declared her lawful husband before the papal court at Avignon. With Joan left out of all of this year's festivities, Bess felt some pity for her, but not all that much.

Isabella clapped her hands. "You look splendid. And put some more pins in your hair if you're worried."

Bess gazed into the full-length glass mirror. For once in her life, she was larger in the chest than she would have preferred. "They can tell I have a bosom! I can't pass as a boy."

"Silly, you're not supposed to. They're supposed to know we are ladies."

"Then I can't see why we can't ride wearing our beautiful new gowns," said Bess. She had had several new ones made for the summer, in the tighter style that was all the rage at court these days, and was a bit resentful that she had not had the chance to show them off properly. Indeed, some ladies wore their new gowns so tight that they had had to sew fox tails within their robes to conceal their rears, but Bess had not been this daring, or desirous of explaining to Hugh the appearance of fox tails in her household accounts, not to mention on her rump.

Isabella sighed, clearly giving Bess up for a lost cause. "It's the sport of it, my dear."

Beside her, Bess's sister-in-law Elizabeth de Berkeley admired her own legs. They were slightly plump and not at all boyish, but Isabella had been running out of willing ladies, so Lizzie, who had just recently consummated her marriage to young Maurice de Berkeley, had been recruited by Bess herself. Pleased with the slenderizing effect of the hose she was wearing, she adjusted them before asking Isabella. "How is the Lady Joan getting on abroad, my lady?"

Joan, the king's second daughter, was on her way to marry Pedro, the heir to the throne of Castile. She was staying in Bordeaux, from whence she was to travel to Bayonne for the ceremony. "She is well," said Isabella shortly, a bit peeved at the conversation turning from her own scheme.

"I would be terrified."

"Of Bordeaux?"

"Of the pestilence," said Lizzie, widening her eyes. "Is his grace the king not concerned? It is running all through the Continent, my father-in-law's men tell him. It is dreadful. People drop dead while you are speaking to them, I hear. And they develop the most horrid black spots in places like—like the groin. And—"

"Enough, Lady Berkeley!" said Isabella. She scowled at Lizzie. "Of course my father has heard of this, but why dwell on it? What an unpleasant topic of conversation."

Bess said diplomatically, "I hear that the King of Castile has a mistress. I wonder if she will be present at the wedding?"

"I would hope that she would stay home," said Isabella, who always enjoyed talk of mistresses and the like, being quite sure that she would never have to put up with one from whatever man she deigned to marry. "But if she does come she will look like an old crow, because Joan has written to me of her wedding garments, and they are magnificent. Are we ready, ladies?"

Outside Windsor Castle, their horses, held by pages, awaited them. Bess mounted her horse and had to admit that breeches made the ride a far more pleasant one. They lined up in orderly rows, Isabella of course by herself at the front in a cap that was richer than the rest of the ladies'. At a sign from Isabella's servant, they trotted out onto the field where the tournament was being held. It was in the same area where Bess's father had been fatally injured, and she had to brush away a tear as it stung her eye.

Following Isabella, they trotted from one end of the field to the other, close enough to hear the spectators' exclamations and laughter as they realized that the riders were not the young men they appeared to be from a distance. Having made two passes, Isabella rode up to the royal dais. Taking garlands off the shoulder where she had been carrying them, she bent and draped one around the neck of the king, who laughed indulgently, and then put a second around the neck of her eldest brother, the Prince of Wales.

The rest of the ladies followed suit with the knights standing near the king. Bess made a point of wreathing her brother William, then looked around for Hugh, a task made somewhat difficult because of her mask, which did not fit very well and was constantly slipping so as to obscure her vision somewhat. Spotting her husband at last, she tossed the garland around his neck while the knights around him applauded. If Hugh recognized his wife, he made no sign of it. To avoid making her identity known, she flung her next wreath around the neck of a Guy Brian, a knight of modest means who had distinguished himself in the king's service, having born his standard at Crécy. Bess had met him at Calais but knew him only superficially.

162

The king stood as the ladies, having completed their task, turned their horses back toward the castle. "Stay—lads," he called.

Isabella shook her head. "We go from whence we came. Fare thee well."

Back by the stables, they dismounted, collected their women's clothing, and went to their separate chambers to dress. Bess with the aid of an attendant had stripped down to her shirt, breeches, and hose when Hugh came in. "My lady," he said as the attendant made her exit, "So it *was* you. I am shocked."

"Oh, it was just a prank of the Lady Isabella's—"

"Shocked to see how fetching my wife is in shirt and breeches," said Hugh, and pulled her against him.

Bess was shocked herself by the intensity, and the originality, of the coupling that followed. As she had physically matured, Hugh had gradually ceased to treat her during love-making as something that might break easily, but this . . . "I'll have a pair of breeches made for me at home if you like," she offered later as she leaned gasping against the wall where Hugh had taken her, to her most intense satisfaction ever.

"Better not." Hugh nuzzled her neck. "Wouldn't want to shock the tenants."

NOT LONG AFTER the Windsor tournament, in late June or July, a thoroughly unremarkable looking vessel pulled into the port of Melcombe Regis. Its cargo was unloaded like that of any other ship; its crew went into the local inns and taverns and brothels to drink and brawl and wench about just like the crew of any other ship. No one would remember what goods were on board, or from exactly whence it came, but no one would ever forget what it had brought, something for which no merchant had bargained or sold.

Four days after the ship dropped anchor, a man in Melcombe became ill, and died. Then another sickened and died. Then another.

The pestilence had come to England.

HUGH AND BESS had scarcely arrived back on their estates when a royal messenger brought the news that the fourteen-year-old Lady Joan had died outside Bordeaux of the pestilence. "Married, indeed," said William Beste as he prepared to lead the household in prayers for the young girl's soul. "But to Death himself, poor child."

ELIZABETH DE BURGH'S CHAPLAIN, preaching in her private chapel at Usk in August, blamed the pestilence on all manner of human folly, but with a most particular emphasis on the tournaments and on the modish clothing that had been so prevalent lately. As the aging lady did not attend tournaments, and her expensive, luxurious robes were all in the fashion of ten years before, she nodded rather complacently as he elaborated on his theme. Her younger houseguests, however, who included Hugh and Bess, looked disconcerted. By the time he was finished, Bess felt almost personally responsible for bringing the pestilence to England.

"Do you really think God would visit this upon us because we wore our robes too tight?" she demanded of Hugh later as they lay in the bed they shared at Usk.

"No. I think God is pleased as anyone else when they flatter pretty little rumps like yours."

"Hugh! I am serious."

"So was I. I've no answers, sweetheart. I can just remember when I was a little boy, there was famine here. There'd been terrible rains, almost constant; nothing could grow. People thought God was displeased then, and finally one day the rain stopped, just as it'd started, without anyone having done anything to please God as far as I could figure out at the time. The peasants who died then were probably no better or worse than those who lived. It all seemed random, somehow. Since then I'm inclined to leave the whys and wherefores to wiser heads than mine."

"It's almost as if I think a soldier must feel, waiting for the enemy to attack."

"No. It's worse, far worse. War's never seemed so simple as it does now. There are rules, strategies, preparations that can be made. This is different. There's nothing we can do but wait and hope we are spared." He stroked her hair and held her closely against him. "That's not entirely true, though. There is one thing we can do, perhaps."

"What?"

"Hide from it, just find someplace to wait out the pestilence. It goes away, they say, sooner or later. Stock one of our castles with as much provisions as possible and have the bare minimum of servants there. Let no one into the castle gates. In other words, act as if we're under siege. But—"

"But you can't do that. I know, Hugh."

He started, and she wondered if he realized what she was realizing, that they had reached the point in their marriage where they knew each other better than anyone else in the entire world. "No, I can't. I've spent nigh on twenty years rebuilding our family's honor. What would happen if I shut myself away from all those who depend on me now? All that trust I've worked to gain would be gone. I'd look as if I were leaving them to their fate. I can't do that, not for my own sake, not for my heir's sake."

"You are right."

"All we can do is carry on as usual." He fidgeted with the ring that Bess had given him. "I said *we*, but it's different in your case. You're so young, and a woman. If you were to shut yourself away—"

"No. We are man and wife, lord and lady. I stand by you, and by our tenants."

"I knew that you would say that," Hugh admitted. "Though I also hoped in a way you wouldn't." He shrugged. "Then it's settled. We take our chances."

HUGH WAS RIGHT; the pestilence was far less predictable an enemy than an army. It would visit one village and leave only a handful of people alive, then skip the next village altogether, then wreak havoc on the next. Bristol, where Hugh had been im-

165

prisoned, was devastated. "Serves them right," Hugh muttered before crossing himself and retreating to their chapel, where Bess later found him on his knees praying dutifully, if not fervently, for the town's deliverance.

London, strangely, had remained untouched for a while, a fact that even encouraged the king to summon Parliament. Bess, planning as always to accompany Hugh to their house in London, prepared for the journey as if all were normal, but no sooner had she made the arrangements than word arrived that the pestilence had become so fierce in London that the king had postponed Parliament. Then he cancelled it altogether.

By the New Year, the whole countryside appeared to be standing still out of fear of the pestilence. Though Hugh and Bess continued to travel between their estates—except in the areas so overrun with disease that no one dared venture there—and to make all visitors welcome, few were on the roads, and those who came to see them on business did not linger after concluding their transactions. Even some of the paupers who regularly arrived at mealtimes stopped coming.

By mid-January the Despensers had returned to Hanley Castle. There, Bess was delighted one day when a draper she had patronized in Bristol appeared with some cloth. Because of the pestilence, he told her, business was so poor there that he had decided to take his goods around to his best customers.

Bess, compassionating the man's plight and not unmindful of the beauty of the rich cloth he showed her, bought almost all he had to offer. With Easter in mind, she had matching robes made for herself and Emma, still her closest friend though no longer her attendant, and had a new set of robes made for Hugh too, in the golden brown color that set off his eyes so nicely. "Very nice," agreed Hugh as they modeled their new garments for each other a few days later. "When shall we get to wear them?"

"Easter, silly. And no sooner," she warned.

"Well, then, take mine off me so I won't be tempted."

Bess obeyed, reading the invitation in Hugh's eyes. They had adjourned to their bed when Bess, caressing Hugh's bare back, brushed her hand against a rough spot on his skin. Hugh made a sound close to a purr. "Scratch there, sweetheart. It itches."

"What is it?"

"Flea bite. They love me, always have. You hardly ever get them, do you?"

"No. They must not find me very tasty."

"You're tasty enough to me," said Hugh, drawing her into his arms.

A FEW DAYS LATER, they had a dinner that was somewhat more grand than the ones they had had lately, as several local officials and their wives had ventured off their manors to join Hugh and Bess at their meal. Bess wished one of the couples had been less bold, for although the husband was an agreeable enough man, the wife, Lady Thornton, was easily the most garrulous woman in Worcester. "Now my head will *really* ache," Hugh grumbled when he heard of the pair's arrival.

"Your head hurts, my love?"

Hugh shrugged and waved toward the accounts he had been going over since the evening before. "Probably all that reading. These days I have to hold everything closer to my eyes than I like to admit." He grinned. "I may have to get some spectacles for reading soon. Do you think you'd still love me in them?"

"I will have to consider the matter," Bess said, trying to picture Hugh in the strange devices.

As the talkative Lady Thornton was the highest ranking of the female guests, she had to be placed next to Bess, who spent the next hour or so nodding politely. She was about to intersperse yet another civil nod when her neighbor suddenly broke off in the middle of describing the robes her daughter had worn for her wedding five years before. "Your lord—is he ill?"

Bess whirled, then blanched. Hugh had dropped his knife on his plate and sat staring at it. Beside him, his own neighbor was saying in a low voice, "My lord? My lord?"

"Hugh!"

Her husband staggered to his feet, knocking the chair backward so hard it crashed to the floor, and stumbled away from the table. Before he could reach the nearest door, he collapsed to his knees and began retching. As Bess followed him, someone screamed, "The pestilence!"

The great hall erupted into chaos as servants, bringing the next course in, were thrust aside and their platters knocked to the floor as the diners rushed from their seats, most to flee the castle, a few to join the knot of people standing by their stricken lord. Bess paid no attention to any of the activity around her. She bent and put her arm around Hugh's shoulders. "I am going to put you to bed," she said when he finally stopped retching. "Can you stand?"

"Please. Go." She shook her head and held him more tightly as he shivered against her. "I hate for you to see me like this. And you'll be ill too. Please, Bessie. Go."

"No, Hugh. You need me to take care of you. If I fall ill, so be it. What is done is done." She stroked Hugh's hair. "Let me take you to your chamber, my love."

Hugh sighed but said nothing. Bess became aware for the first time of the others around her as a squire touched her shoulder. "We'll carry him there, my lady."

She nodded and stood aside as the squire and another man hoisted an unresisting Hugh off the floor. Someone—she had no idea who—took her own arm and helped her up the winding stairs to Hugh's chamber.

Alice the laundress, though well into her sixties, still remained in Hugh's service, having resisted Hugh's attempts to have her live in comfortable retirement on one of his manors. Though she had reluctantly ceded her heaviest duties to a younger woman, she had made herself indispensable in sundry other ways, as she did now by helping Bess guide Hugh to a stool and to begin undressing him. "Jesus help us," she whispered as she removed Hugh's shirt. "My poor sweet lamb."

There under Hugh's armpits, smaller than a penny but unmistakable, were the black swellings that were the tokens of the pestilence. As everybody stared at this confirmation of their worst fears, Hugh himself finally broke the silence. "It looks as if I'll be the first Hugh le Despenser in four generations to die in bed," he said. "It's sadly overrated, if you ask me."

Bess gave him the smile he wanted. With the help of Alice, who was weeping noiselessly, she assisted Hugh into bed, realizing as she arranged the sheets around him that he was feverish. If the pestilence took its usual course, Hugh would soon be delirious. She looked around and saw with something approaching relief that Hugh's confessor was there. "Shrive him now before he is too ill to manage it," she said in a more commanding tone than she had intended.

Beste nodded. "I shall. I must go prepare the Sacrament, my lady."

Bess pressed her cheek against Hugh's as they waited. He was warmer to the touch than he had been just minutes before. Already, it was plain he was having difficulty focusing his thoughts. "My will's made, Bess. It's in the hands of—" He frowned, trying to recall the name of his own steward, who was standing not far off.

"I know where to find it, my love."

"Is Beste coming back?"

"Yes. Of course." But she wondered if he had taken the opportunity to run away as so many did when the pestilence struck.

Beste, however, returned presently. Bess gave her place to him and watched from a distance as Hugh managed to take communion and to confess his sins. Twice Hugh's confession was interrupted when he coughed up blood. When Beste had finished, he said, "I shall stay, my lady. It is my duty as his confessor and his friend."

Bess's eyes filled with tears, and she hated herself for having thought the man might desert Hugh.

But with one person ill, others would surely fall victim to the pestilence as well. In the same authoritative voice as before, Bess heard herself giving orders to Hugh's steward. He was to let it be known that any person who helped her with Hugh and with the other sufferers would be paid handsomely, as would those who continued to discharge their duties as before. Anyone who left Hanley Castle during this crisis would get nothing.

"Termagant," murmured Hugh. He managed one last smile. "That was one way of chasing off Lady Thornton, you'll admit."

By the time dusk fell, Bess, tending Hugh with the help of Alice, heard through the handful of servants who dared to enter the chamber that several others in the castle had fallen ill, and that the pestilence had reached the tenants of Hanley as well. She paid little attention, though, for Hugh was delirious, sometimes crying out in agony, sometimes trying to fight off imaginary opponents, sometimes muttering vacantly.

The next morning, after a long night of agony for both Hugh and Bess, a knock sounded at the door. "Come in," Bess said dully, then turned. "Emma!" She entered Emma's waiting arms. "He's so ill," she whispered. "Nothing I can do eases him. Nothing."

Emma let her cry for a few minutes, then gently disengaged herself and looked at the bed where Hugh lay groaning. "I came here to help. Tell me what I can do for you."

"Wait! Your husband and children."

"They have no need of me now. They died this morning." Bess made a move to comfort her friend with a touch, and Emma shook her head. "Say no more about it, or I shall break down."

As time passed, Hugh became more agitated, crying out and even trying to rise from his bed. Bess had heard the stories of pestilence sufferers jumping from windows, their derangement having given them strength to fight off all who might stop them. It would break her heart to do so, but if tying Hugh to his bed like a madman was necessary to keep him safe— "Bess!" her husband cried.

She bent instantly and touched his face. "My love, I'm right here."

"Bess," Hugh whispered contentedly. His face relaxed and he was quiet.

Emma said, "Your voice comforts him. Perhaps reading to him would help."

"Get my Book of Hours," Bess said to a servant.

Throughout the rest of the day and night, Bess and Emma read to Hugh from whatever book happened to be at hand—Bess's Book of Hours, a romance, even the household account books that Hugh had been reviewing before he was stricken. Alice too took her turn. She could not read, of course, so she told him tales instead, some so bawdy that Bess, hearing snatches of them occasionally, would blush despite herself. Hugh gave no sign he understood any of what was said to him, but he seemed far less agitated, and for that Bess would drone on and on until she became hoarse or started nodding off over the pages. Then Emma or Alice would take over. William Beste, stopping in now and then as he made the rounds between Hugh and the others who had fallen ill, read also on occasion, but to no good effect. His male voice had no soothing effect on the patient; it seemed to be female voices alone that calmed him.

It was at dinner time the next day that Bess began reading to Hugh from a chronicle that Hugh must have had copied for personal reasons, for as Bess was reading to him of the Battle of Evesham, she came to a passage about a Hugh le Despenser. "Today we shall all drink—"

"From one cup," came a faint voice. Bess started and looked down at Hugh, who had opened his eyes. "My great-grandfather. I wanted to be like him. Loyal and brave."

"You were, my love." *Were.* The tears started to run down her face.

"I thought I heard Emma's voice. Is she here?"

Emma came over, looked at Bess, and reading permission in her eyes, bent and kissed Hugh on the forehead. "I am here, Hugh."

"Emmy. You are well?"

"Yes, Hugh. Very well."

"Your family?"

"Very well too."

"Alice?"

"Here, lamb. I've not washed your shirts for twenty some years to leave you now."

Hugh smiled, then closed his eyes. For a moment, Bess thought that he had slipped away from her. Then he whispered, "Bess."

"Yes, Hugh?"

"Sweetheart. Promise me something?"

She knew what he wanted. "Yes. I will never remarry, Hugh. I will take a vow of chastity. I—"

He almost chuckled. "Listen first. Do. Remarry."

"Remarry! How dare you ask—"

"Bad time to bicker," Hugh said weakly. He grimaced, then said. "A waste. Too young, too sweet and fair. Please, Bess. Promise me."

"All right," Bess said almost grudgingly. "But I won't like it."

"Same old Bess."

She could hardly understand the words he was saying before his voice trailed off. To ease her aching back, Bess stood up. She gazed at her husband. The torments the dowager queen and her lover had visited upon his father's and his grandfather's bodies could hardly have been worse than those the pestilence had wreaked upon Hugh, she thought. The pustules had spread over his body, which was covered with bluish splotches; his flesh was wasted; his breath stank. Three days before he had been a handsome man, how handsome Bess had never realized until all was destroyed. Bess sat again. She placed her hand over her husband's and said into his ear, "I love you. You were my perfect, gentle knight."

His lip twitched upward and he tried to grasp her hand. In a moment or two, he was gone.

9

April 1349 to January 1350

At Windsor Castle, Will, Earl of Salisbury, preened in his new robe, powdered with little blue garters. "How do you like it, sister?"

"It suits you well," Bess said absently, though she was not even looking at her brother but at her wedding ring. Recalling herself, she added, "Particularly with your new beard."

Will grinned and stroked it. Unconsciously, he ran his hand over his leg to make certain that the garter just below his knee had not disappeared during the few minutes that had passed since he last checked it.

Bess had a habit these days of talking to Hugh in her head, and she'd had a fine conversation with him about the king's ridiculous new scheme, which as far as Bess could tell was simply another excuse for men to dress up in matching robes and joust. "Order of the Garter?" she had asked Hugh. "Could he have found a sillier name?"

"Order of the Breech-cloth," Hugh had suggested. Then, "Now, now, Bess. Remember the motto. *Honi soit qui mal y pense.*"

Bess scowled. Yet she could not deny that if Hugh had been alive and wearing one of the silly garters on his leg, she'd probably not found it ridiculous at all.

She would have gladly forsaken the St. George's Day festivities at Windsor had not Will begged her to come. Their mother, no longer in the best of health, was disinclined to travel these days, and with the Pope still at the business of deciding whether Joan of Kent was Will's wife or Thomas's, Will had had no lady to bear him company. So Bess, being free, had accepted the king's invitation to come to Windsor, even though it meant traveling through a landscape where many of the inns were shuttered and where entire towns were empty of inhabitants. For although one couldn't tell it from anything at Windsor, save for the mourning robes of Bess and a handful of others, the pestilence had not yet abated.

Weeks before, Hugh and Bess had taken one last journey together, Bess riding on the palfrey Hugh had given her on their wedding day, Hugh inside a wooden coffin, jouncing in a cart traveling to Tewkesbury Abbey, Hugh's last resting place of choice. There, Bess at least had had the relief of seeing Hugh's body properly cared for: encased in lead, enclosed in a heavy oak coffin, and laid just north of the high altar, surrounded by candles provided by Bess. With the pestilence keeping so many on their own lands, Hugh's funeral mass had been sparsely attended outside Bess's own household, save for the monks, some paupers who received alms for the occasion, and a few of the braver tenants, but the simple, dignified service was one that Bess thought would have pleased him. And when times were better—if times were ever better—she would raise a beautiful monument to his memory, she had promised Hugh as the last strains of the monks' chanting died away.

Emma would have no tomb. Hours after Hugh died, she had fallen ill. Bess had nursed her to the last, but to no avail. Bess had had her friend's body dressed in the fine Easter robes Bess had ordered for her, wrapped in fine linen, and taken to the mass grave outside Hanley's village church, where the bodies of Emma's husband and children had already been placed with those of a score of other villagers.

A dozen of the household at Hanley Castle had died, including the faithful Alice and William Beste. With Hugh gone, Bess had helped tend them all, expecting, and partly hoping, each time she covered yet another dead face that someone would soon be doing the same for her. But she had remained in perfect health. It was grief, not illness, that had caused her to grow markedly thinner and to drag herself around with a weary step.

Almost before Hugh was cold—or at least it seemed to Bess—the king's escheators had arrived to take charge of his land, Hugh's heir, his brother Edward's oldest boy, being but twelve years old. Bess knew this was necessary, as Hugh, like most of the barons, had held his lands of the crown, and they would have to be administered by men of the king's choosing until Edward came of age. Still, she mightily resented the presence of the men swarming over Hugh's estates: poking through Hugh's account books, measuring his land, even counting up his sheep. Most odious of all was their habit of looking sidelong at Bess's belly, to see if she was bearing Hugh's child. Even after Bess herself was in no possible doubt—her monthly course started a few days after her arrival at Tewkesbury—she said nothing to enlighten them. "Let them figure it out for themselves," she muttered to Hugh.

By the end of February she was back at Hanley Castle, where the king had deemed she should stay until her dower was assigned to her. Even there she was beset by the escheators, though, and it was perhaps as much to escape them as to be with her brother that she had decided to travel to Windsor in April. Besides, Will had reminded her, her presence there was bound to speed along the dower process.

Will was now looking at her critically. "Are you wearing that to dinner?"

Bess glanced at her mourning robes. Somewhat ill-fitting to begin with, they had grown more so as her appetite continued to lessen. "My new man does the best he can, but he lacks the skill and speed of Michael Taylor. He died a few days after Hugh."

"Maybe mine could help. Or perhaps the Lady Isabella—"

"I don't care for help," Bess snapped. Seeing her brother's hurt expression, she said more mildly, "I don't need it in any case. I could have warts on my nose and foul breath and still not want for male company. Every man here who is unmarried or widowed, or who has a son or a brother or a nephew or a friend who is unmarried or widowed, or a wife who is ailing, has been paying particular attention to me. They know more about the lands I will receive, down to the last hedgerow, than I do."

"Well, one can't blame them for trying. I'd try for you if you weren't my sister." Will sat heavily on the bed, Hugh's traveling bed that he had willed to Bess. "And it appears that I will soon be on the market for a wife myself."

Thomas Holland, like Will, had been made a Knight of the Garter. Rather tactlessly, Bess thought, the king had invited the bone of their contention to the festivities as well. Joan's months of relative isolation had not lessened her beauty in the slightest, and though she had conducted herself as demurely as the subject of papal marital litigation ought to, she was still the center of attention. Even the king could not keep his eyes off her, and his eldest son, Edward, was no better. "You think the Pope will rule against you?"

"My proctor wasn't hopeful. And what if he rules for me? Could Joan and I ever hope to live together normally?"

Bess had been wondering this herself. She patted her brother on the arm. "Joan has always been flighty, but I do believe her to be honorable. If she were to be adjudged your wife, I think she would abide by the ruling. But perhaps it might be just as well if Holland gets her. You can start afresh."

"Yes, with a girl far too young to have got herself into such a situation. One who's been in a convent, perhaps. A moated convent."

"And she never bore you children. Perhaps your next marriage will be more blessed."

"It's a thought. What of you, sister? Shall you remarry?"

She shook her head. "It is far too soon to think of it."

"Well, shall I escort you to dinner?"

BESS WATCHED as a group of dancers twirled around in a carol, growing wilder by the moment. Merry as the festivities had been five years before, when Bess had flirted with her king, they were downright raucous now.

She was standing in the same hall in which she had stood those five years ago. Edward had built a round house especially to hold the Round Table he had announced so grandly in 1344, but no feast had ever been held there, the demands on the king's purse having brought the work to a halt long ago. Bess wondered idly if the project would ever be resumed. She doubted it. Why bother to build when all those in this room could be dead within days if the pestilence came to Windsor or to any royal castle it pleased?

A man passing through the crowd greeted her, and Bess stared back coolly. Bartholomew de Burghersh, yet another new Knight of the Garter, was in excellent spirits these days, though he was trying to contain them around Bess. Just a couple of years ago, he'd arranged to have his eldest daughter, Elizabeth, marry young Edward le Despenser. Instead of the moderately prosperous young boy whom Burghersh had bargained for, he'd ended up with the future Lord of Glamorgan, thanks to the pestilence and Bess's failure to bear Hugh a child. Bess was not surprised to see that twelve-year-old Edward had not accompanied Burghersh to the Garter festivities, though she knew from Anne le Despenser that the boy loved to watch jousting and constantly talked of the day when he could take the field as a knight, like his father and like his uncle. Sir Bartholomew was not about to risk losing his rich little son-in-law to the pestilence by having him travel about, she thought bitterly.

Bess saw him glance, as surreptitiously as possible, at her belly. In a carrying voice, she announced, "You need not worry yourself, Sir Bartholomew. I am not with Hugh's child. Your prize catch is quite safe."

Ignoring Burghersh's protestations, she pushed through the crowd, not bothering to apologize as she trod on toes and even on the hand of a man who was bending over. Reaching its fringes at last, she found herself face to face with Joan of Kent, standing decorously with a couple of lady friends. Looking into Joan's beautiful face, her rosy complexion contrasting with her own sallow looks, Bess suddenly felt a flash of pure hatred. Why could not God have done the most convenient thing and taken Thomas Holland instead of Hugh?

Appalled at the level she was sinking to, wishing death upon a man who had done her no harm and who might well be Joan's lawful wedded husband, she turned without having spoken a word to her former close companion and continued to press through the throng. Free of the crowd at last, she stopped to catch her breath only to find Guy Brian beside her. "What the devil do you want?" she demanded.

"Well, for one thing I was interested in knowing the identity of the lady who almost broke my hand."

He held it out to her, and Bess flushed with remorse. "I beg your pardon."

"And I also thought you might be ill and in need of assistance."

"I am not with child, and I do not have the pestilence; I know well the signs of both. So no one at Windsor has anything to fear from me." Her own rudeness took her aback. "Sir Guy, I do beg your pardon again. I—"

Instead of finishing her sentence, she began crying. Sir Guy hesitated, then drew her against his shoulder as she wept. "There," he said gently after she had finally quieted. "Better?"

She nodded and drew back. "I feel so foolish."

"I think perhaps you needed to do that."

"Sir Guy, I do apologize for your hand."

"Nothing is broken, though you have a good strong foot, my lady."

"I suppose I should beg pardon of Sir Bartholomew and my sister-in-law Joan too."

"Indeed? You were quite busy in there, it seems."

"I am not usually horrid like that, truly. It is just—" She dabbed at her nose. "It was a mistake coming here; I should have stayed away. I shall go to my chamber before I insult anyone else or break down and cry again."

"Do you have a page to take you there, my lady?"

"Somewhere." She looked around. "He is the son of a neighbor who died. He has much to learn yet about his duties."

"Mine shall find him for you." He gestured to a boy who was standing at some distance from him. "Find Lady Despenser's page for her. She wishes to retire for the evening. Here, Lady Despenser. Sit and rest."

She settled on the bench he indicated.

"I heard, of course, of Sir Hugh's death. Please accept my condolences. He was a fine knight and will be sorely missed."

"Indeed he will be." She sat in silence for a while, grateful that Sir Guy was not one to chatter idly just for the sake of hearing his own voice. Then she surprised herself by saying, "I know many have lost much more than I have—all of their relations and friends, instead of one man. Yet telling myself that makes it no easier to bear. And then I feel thoroughly ashamed of myself for wallowing in self-pity, even anger as I was just now. I was so vile in there." She thought of young Edward le Despenser, who had written her a very kind note after Hugh's death, and sniffled. It was not the poor boy's fault that he was Hugh's heir.

"If you wish I will make your apologies for you."

"Thank you. I think I should make them myself in the morning, though."

"May I say something without sounding trivial, I hope? I know how it is to grieve, my lady, but I also know how it is to recover. There will come a day when your heart will be lighter, though you may not believe it now."

A boom of laughter, obviously the king's, came from inside the hall. "And there is another thing. How can he make so merry?"

"My lady?"

"The king's daughter died less than a twelvemonth ago. So many have died. How can he laugh as if nothing is the matter? I cannot understand it. I never thought he could have such a hard heart."

Guy said, "I don't think his heart is hard, my lady. He knows as well as the rest of us do that life may never be the same, and that many households have suffered grievously. But carrying on as best he can gives him heart, and I think it gives the rest of us heart too."

"It gives me none."

"You only recently lost a husband whom I think you loved very much, Lady Despenser. I remember seeing the two of you in Calais together and thinking what a fine couple you made, and how happy you appeared together. My wife was ailing then. It was bitter to see."

"I did not mean to give you pain."

"Hardly your fault, my lady." He half smiled as another roar came from the great hall. "At least you have to admit it's more congenial than the Flagellants; have you heard of them? They travel from town to town on the Continent, scourging themselves on the back. It's their way of atoning for all of our sins, they say."

"Why, that sounds almost blasphemous."

"Blasphemous, and painful too. Give me a joust and dancing any day."

Bess smiled. "Here is my page," she said almost regretfully, for she had found something soothing in Sir Guy's company. If she had to sit beside any man the next day, Sir Guy would be the best, she thought later, wincing as her young maid—a newly orphaned girl who like her page owed her position in the household to Bess's charity, not to any skill in performing her duties—clumsily braided Bess's hair for the night.

The next day, she woke to a royal summons. Obeying it, she found the king in his chamber, relaxing with the queen. "Lady Despenser. Our clerks will soon finish this business about your dower. You may swear your homage to us now, and also that you will not remarry without our license, of course."

Bess knelt, rather glad that she was not having to perform the ritual in front of a crowd of courtiers, and swore her oath to the king, who then helped her rise. "We were grieved to hear about Sir Hugh, my lady. He served us well." Edward indicated his own garter, a duplicate of the one Will was so assiduous in checking. "Pity. Had he lived, he might have come to wear one of these."

"He would have been most honored to hear you speak of him so, your grace." Probably he would have been, Bess supposed, given the unaccountable stock that men put into such things.

"Well, Burghersh says that Sir Hugh's nephew Edward is a promising lad. But come now, Bess, your father and I were old friends. There's no reason for us to be so formal. Since you've arrived, I've taken care to put several likely men in your path. Do any of them suit?"

"Your grace?"

The king shrugged. "I know it's far too early to think of marrying any of them, but there's no harm in looking to see who's available, now is there? Of course, I must approve the match, but within reason, you can pick for yourself. It's certainly not too early to narrow the field. With your wealth and that pretty—"

"Your grace. It is *you* who has encouraged these men to inspect me like a horse at the fair?"

"My dear, it's a two-sided transaction, you see. They inspect you. You inspect them. Indeed, it's you who should be doing most of the inspecting, because their minds are made up. All of them want to marry you, whereas you can pick only one of them. Or none, of course. But that would be a waste."

"Ned!" Philippa interjected. "I do not think Lady Despenser is ready for your matchmaking yet."

The king cheerfully ignored her. "What did you think of Guy Brian? He wasn't one of my original choices, but I hear that he was talking to you last night. Oh, yes, my dear, kings find about these things. Now there's a brave, loyal man I'd like to reward with a good marriage."

"I will marry no man until I am ready. If I ever am ready, that is."

"Of course, Lady Despenser," said Philippa, frowning at her husband. "There is no need to rush. Never mind Ned. It is simply that he wants to see you settled and comfortable again, for your father's sake."

"Out of that blasted black and into some pretty colors," the king said. "And dancing." He grinned at her. "You dance quite well, as I recall. And if I'm not mistaken, you're quite accomplished at kissing also."

Bess was blushing and searching for a suitable reply, if there indeed was one with Philippa present, when a messenger entered the room and asked to see the king privately. The two of them withdrew into an inner chamber, leaving the women alone. "You must excuse Ned, Lady Despenser. The pestilence has had an odd effect on some people, and in his case it has made him unseemly jocular at times."

They had barely embarked upon small talk, which Philippa was tactful enough to ensure did not involve matrimony for Bess, when the king walked slowly back into the room.

"Lady Despenser," he said in a voice very different from the one he had used just minutes ago, "we have had sad news that pertains to you and your brothers and sisters. Your lady mother has been ill—with the pestilence, we are grieved to say. She is dead."

IN SPITE OF EVERYTHING, Bess's world had returned to some state of normalcy by the following January. As spring had changed to summer and summer to fall, fewer and fewer reports came of people dying of the pestilence. Slowly, guests began to return to Bess's great hall, and Bess herself, who had been drifting back and forth between her Welsh estates and Hanley Castle, accepting invitations to visit now and then but merely going through the motions of her existence, found it harder and harder to ignore the life around her.

For there was life around her, despite the fresh graves in every churchyard, the fallow fields, and the abandoned houses that littered the countryside. Widowed tenants of Bess's married other bereaved tenants, and already a few of the brides were big with child. Tenants arrived to lease houses, like Emma's, left vacant by the pestilence. Her awkward tailor and her awkward maid, more sure of their duties these days, married each other, and her maid's burgeoning belly soon proved that they were not too awkward to have figured out the intricacies of the marriage bed. A new chaplain took Beste's place at Hanley Castle. There had even been fighting between the English and the French again.

"So I understand the Pope's decision went against your brother?" Elizabeth de Burgh asked Bess, newly arrived at Usk in January.

Bess nodded. "Will was chagrined, I think, but he adjusted fairly quickly. I think he must have been expecting it, really. He is planning to marry little Elizabeth Mohun. Her father was made a Garter Knight along with Will. She's all of six years old, so I suppose there won't be a previous marriage in her case."

"Lord help us if there is," said Elizabeth de Burgh. "But starting afresh, that's the best thing he can do. And what of you, my dear? Are you ready to start anew? Has anyone asked for your hand?"

"Not in so many words. But I have had several men find themselves astray in Wales in the past months."

"I'm not in the least bit surprised."

"I have also seen that Guy Brian I told you about when I was here over the summer. Some of Hugh's estates have been put into his keeping, and that brings him onto my own estates for business on occasion. And I believe the king would like to put me in his keeping as well. He is high in the king's favor, and Will is always passing on the king's praises of him to me. I imagine the king encourages him to do so."

"And what do you think of Sir Guy?"

"I like him well enough."

"Well enough to marry him?"

Bess shrugged impatiently. "Everyone wants me to remarry. The king, Will, my sisters—and of course Hugh told me before he died that I should. Sir Guy is a kind man, and Hugh spoke well of him on occasion. I could live with him, I suppose, but—"

"But what, child?"

"I just wish I had some sort of a sign."

"A bolt of lightning?"

"Just *something*," Bess said, a little miffed. "How do women choose their spouses? I've never had to do it."

"Well, you could ask that pretty Joan; she chose Holland, after all. Or you could ask me. I chose my second husband."

"How?"

"I liked him, and he was a good man. And I knew that if I did not choose him, the second Edward would choose someone for me who might not be to my taste. As he did when I was widowed not many months after I married my second husband." She sighed. "It was a happy marriage while it lasted, child." She smiled. "And Theobald was persistent, which also helped his cause."

"Well, Sir Guy hasn't been that. He has said nothing about marriage."

"Oh?" Elizabeth de Burgh stood. "My, this cold weather makes my bones ache. Perhaps Sir Guy will be more forthcoming when he comes here."

"Here?"

"He is expected tomorrow."

GUY BRIAN INDEED ARRIVED the next day and was put by Bess's side at dinner, where he and Bess made stiff, awkward conversation about the state of the nation. Bess was ready to scream with relief when the last course was served and Elizabeth de Burgh rose from her splendid chair, signaling to the company that they were free to leave themselves. "Shall we go for a walk around the bailey, my lady?"

It was bone-chillingly cold outside, and the bailey of Usk Castle was hardly a point of interest, but Bess agreed and sent her man for her warmest cloak. When both Guy and Bess were suitably attired, they entered the bailey and began walking in a circular path. "I believe you can guess why I am here, my lady." She nodded. "The king has approved of what I am going to ask you, which is to be my wife."

"I thought so."

"You're under no compulsion, my lady. You can refuse if you wish." Bess smiled, and Guy went on, "I know, I know, that isn't what I should be saying. I should be telling you of my virtues, in the most humble way possible, and extolling your beauty and grace. And I do find you beautiful and graceful. But I'm not much with words, and I don't want you marrying me because you feel that you've been placed under duress."

"No, I feel no duress. The king has made it clear that he wishes the match, but I know he is not a man to bully a woman into taking a husband she doesn't want."

"Indeed, we are lucky in our king."

"Sir Guy, there is something you must realize. I am barren. In all of my years of marriage with Hugh, I never quickened with child."

"I have known women not to conceive with one man and then to conceive with another." Bess frowned, and Guy hastened to add, "Mind you, my lady, it is no aspersion upon the man's— abilities, might I say. But I have seen such things. And you were very young when you came to Sir Hugh, and are young still. It may be that God would bless our union with children were you to marry me. But if not—well, I have two daughters of my own to inherit my estates if we are not so fortunate as to have a son."

"Daughters?"

"Good girls, I think you would find them. They miss their mother, as of course do I. I think they would adjust well to a stepmother." He smiled. "They aren't so old as to be jealous of what a pretty stepmother they would be getting if you were to accept me as your husband. There, now I've made you a proper compliment, you see."

"How old are they?"

"Elizabeth is ten, Mary eight. We call Elizabeth by her full name, so there would be no confusion with a Bess in the household."

He fell silent, perhaps thinking that he had been too hasty in anticipating a favorable response. They began their second turn around the bailey, Bess still waiting for a sign. But as Elizabeth de Burgh had asked, what heavenly manifestation did she expect? Wasn't it enough, perhaps, that a man she knew to be of good character, approved by the king and held in esteem by all who knew him, had come here to ask her to be his wife?

All around her, those whose lives had been shattered by the pestilence had found the will and strength to begin again. Should she be no less brave than the most lowly of her tenants? Why, she was the daughter of the Earl of Salisbury, who'd risked his very life for the king that long-ago night at Nottingham Castle. She owed it to him—and to Hugh and all of the others who had died of the pestilence—to show a little daring. They had faced death or the threat of it without flinching; she could at least face life with the same courage.

Bess took a deep breath. "I will marry you, Sir Guy."

As the words left her lips in a whisper, relief surged through her body. Hugh had been right; she did not wish to live the rest of her life alone. It would be good to be a wife again, and perhaps Guy's daughters might be in need of mothering. And who could say? Maybe God in His grace would let her bear this man the children she had never been able to give to Hugh. "And who knows? The king might build that Round Table of his after all."

"My lady? I did not catch all of what you said."

"Only the first part was of any consequence. I will be pleased to be your wife."

Guy took her hand "Then I thank you, my lady." He stepped a little closer to her. "Shall we try out each other?"

She nodded a little nervously, and he drew her in for a kiss, one that was light at first and gradually became more insistent. It was easier, and more pleasant, kissing Sir Guy than Bess had expected. After they drew apart at last, she was well content to let her husband-to-be kiss her a second time, and then even to kiss him back very thoroughly, before they went inside the castle to tell Elizabeth de Burgh their news.

Author's Note

Bess and Guy Brian married some time in 1350 and had at least four children together, three boys and a girl, before Bess's death in 1359 at Ashley, a manor she had held in jointure with Hugh. Bess was buried next to Hugh in Tewkesbury Abbey. Guy, who never remarried and who survived Bess by thirty-one years, had his own tomb constructed opposite that of Hugh and Bess. Both canopied tombs, among the finest of their time, can still be seen today.

The Lady Chapel at Tewkesbury Abbey that Bess and Hugh visit before their wedding was torn down during Henry VIII's dissolution of the monasteries. The details of Eleanor de Clare's tomb are purely fictitious, as no description of it or even of its location in Tewkesbury survives.

Guy Brian enjoyed a successful and varied career in Edward III's service and was created a Knight of the Garter in 1370. One of his Garter companions was Hugh's heir and eldest nephew, Edward, who was named to the Order in 1361. Edward, regarded by the chronicler Froissart as a model of chivalry, had a shining but sadly brief career; he died in 1375, aged only thirty-nine.

Bess and Guy's oldest son, naturally named Guy, married Alice de Bures, whose household records form the basis of a study by ffiona Swabey entitled *Medieval Gentlewoman: Life in a Widow's Household in the Later Middle Ages*.

Joan of Kent's husband Thomas Holland died in 1360, Joan having borne him five children. After his death, Joan married

Edward III's eldest son, the Black Prince, in what is usually considered to be a love match. Their eldest son, Edward, died young; their second son, Richard, ascended the throne as Richard II. Joan died in 1385, reputedly of grief when Richard refused to show mercy to his half-brother John Holland, who had murdered Ralph Stafford.

Bess's brother William died in 1397, having had one son by his second wife. Tragically, William accidentally killed his son at a tournament in 1382. William was survived by his wife and was buried at Bisham Abbey, the resting place of his father

Some readers may have wondered why neither Joan of Kent nor Bess's mother, the Countess of Salisbury, drops her famous garter to be picked up by Edward III. Sadly, this well-known legend is now regarded by historians as apocryphal, though the exact origins of the Order of the Garter and its motto remain obscure.

Edward III never did resume work on his Round Table house, the Order of the Garter having become the preeminent chivalric institution of his day. The house was torn down during remodeling around 1358 to 1361. Its remains were excavated in 2006.

Hugh's mistress, Emma, is a fictitious character, as is his laundress, Alice. Hugh's cause of death on February 8, 1349, is unknown, but it seems likelier than not that he was a victim of the Black Death, called simply "the pestilence" at the time.

Estimates of the death toll from the pestilence of 1348–49 vary, but the most common figure is that a third of the population perished. The fortitude with which the survivors bore this catastrophe and rebuilt their lives is remarkable. Philip Ziegler in *The Black Death* has commented on the stoicism displayed by so many at the time: "With his friends and relations dying in droves around him, with labour lacking to till the fields and care for the cattle, with every kind of human intercourse rendered perilous by the possibility of infection, the medieval Englishman obstinately carried on in his wonted way."

Printed in the United States
105914LV00002B/126/A

9 780615 171876